DARBY'S DECISION

LAURA SCOTT

READSCAPE PUBLISHING, LLC

Copyright © 2021 by Laura Iding

All rights reserved.

No part of this book may be reproduced in any form or by any electronic or mechanical means, including information storage and retrieval systems, without written permission from the author, except for the use of brief quotations in a book review.

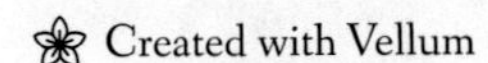

CHAPTER ONE

Six years sober.

Darby Walsh took a moment to let that sink in, before kissing her five-year-old son, Leo, on the top of his head. "See you later, kiddo. Be good for Oma."

"I will." Leo slid a sideways glance at Edith Schroeder, the woman who had not only supported Darby during her stay at the halfway house after she'd finished rehab but who had continued to provide a loving home for both Darby and Leo.

Darby wouldn't be alive and living with Leo in Knoxville today if not for Edith's support. She looked at the woman she loved like a mother. "I'm working the zip line today, so if you call and I can't answer right away, you'll know why."

"Not a problem. Leo and I are going to the park after breakfast." Edith smiled down at the rambunctious towhead. "We'll be fine."

"Great. See you both later." Darby left the side-by-side townhouse and headed to the Great Outdoor Adventure Park where she worked as a guide. She was proud of her sobriety and normally didn't dwell on the multitude of mistakes she'd made in the past.

But lately she'd been thinking about her foster siblings, especially Hailey. For so long her focus was centered on providing a stable life for herself and Leo. Now she was becoming distracted by thoughts of reconnecting with Hailey and the other foster kids. Sawyer, Trent, Jayme, Caitlyn, and Cooper.

Oh, how she'd crushed on Cooper.

Darby arrived at the park and quickly headed inside the main building. The weather was warm and humid for mid-June, but their schedules were jam-packed thanks to the summer tourists.

"Hey, Darby," Teddy greeted her. Teddy was young, barely twenty-one, and followed her around like a puppy. She'd tried to let him down gently, she had no time for or interest in a relationship, especially not with Teddy, but he'd continued to work his schedule to be paired up with her. "I'm working the zip lines with you today."

She suppressed a sigh. Of course he was. "Great. Let's check the gear and set up."

The park had seven different zip lines set at various heights and lengths. Darby loved zip-lining, the freedom of flying. Yet she took safety measures seriously, especially since she had Leo to consider. After methodically checking the cables, straps, and vests, she was satisfied they were good to go.

The first tour came up fifteen minutes later. A family of five, two adults and three teenagers.

Darby gave her usual lecture reiterating the rules and stressing safety. As always, she would go across the zip line first to show the group how things worked, and so she could stay on the other platform to help bring them in. Teddy would remain here to assist in getting their guests suited up and to secure their straps with the buckle clasps before sending them across to her.

"The key is to pull this strap here to slow down when you reach the other side," Darby explained. "But don't worry, I'll be there to grab you."

She tightened the strap on her helmet and clipped her vest and straps to the cable. "See you on the other side!" She pushed off.

Halfway across the cable, she heard a popping sound. Then the cable fell away, and she was free-falling.

Fingers of panic locked around her throat. At some level she heard the screams from the guests behind her, but there wasn't a moment to waste on them. Seeing the canopy of a large tree beneath her, she hoped for the best as she landed on the leafy branches. Her momentum threatened to push her off the other side, dropping into the valley below, but she somehow managed to grab onto a tree branch with both hands, hanging on with every ounce of strength she possessed. She was lying on her stomach, hoping the tree branches beneath her would hold up under the pressure.

"DARBY!" Teddy screamed her name from the platform behind her. But her position was such that she didn't want to move. She could barely breathe for fear of falling the rest of the way to the ground.

"We're getting out of here," a woman shrieked. "This isn't safe!"

Darby couldn't reassure them even if she wanted to. Never in her life had she experienced something like this. These cables were strong enough to hold up to 250 pounds, and she weighed in at 125. She'd worked this park for the past several years without an issue.

What on earth had happened?

Moving very carefully, she turned her head to look behind her. She was too far away to see what had happened to the cable anchored into the pole holding up the platform. Teddy had gotten the family of five down to the ground and was hopefully getting their manager to call the fire department to rescue her. Thankfully, the first zip line is the shortest and the lowest of them, or she knew she would have suffered severe injuries.

Still could if the tree branches beneath her gave way before she was rescued.

A flash of movement below caught her eye. A man moving through the trees. She frowned, a chill washing over her. Had the cable been tampered with on purpose?

No, she was letting her imagination run away with her.

Wasn't she?

The park was full of tourists. *Get a grip, Darby*, she silently admonished. There was no reason for anyone to hurt her. Maybe in the past, in the days when she was associated with drugs, but not anymore.

The sound of a cracking tree branch made her freeze. How long would it take the fire department to get here? She tried to peer through the dense leaves to get an estimate of where the larger branches were. She'd hiked the wooden trails more times than she could count, but she hadn't spent much time climbing trees.

Not even as a kid. Living with the Preacher, a horrible evil man who'd physically and verbally abused her and her foster siblings, had not included fun activities like tree climbing. Quite the opposite. They'd knelt for hours on end listening to the Preacher yell and scream at them for being sinners, warning of God's fury. They'd slept in the cellar and were only allowed to do household chores and homework from Ruth, the Preacher's wife, who'd homeschooled them.

Another branch gave way beneath her, and she tightened her grip on the branch that had broken her fall. No point in thinking about the past now. She needed to be rescued and quickly. Leo needed her.

And she needed him.

"Hang in there, Darby," Teddy called. "They're coming soon."

"I'm doing my best. What happened?"

"It looks like there is damage in the pole around the spot where the cable was bolted in," Teddy said.

Damage? Like someone tampered with it on purpose? "How did we miss that?"

"I think the damage was camouflaged in some way." Teddy's voice sounded muffled now as if he was facing the opposite way. "Kent is pretty upset."

Kent Jacobs was their boss and the manager of the Great Outdoor Adventure Park. He was a decent guy, although he generally focused on making a profit. She knew he was likely more upset about losing the revenue from the zip line than her fall.

The next hour seemed to go by in the blink of an eye. The firetruck arrived, and a fireman emerged in her line of vision. He stood in a large bucket that was within arm's reach.

"Ma'am? I need you to take my hand."

"I'm not sure I can do that," she confessed. Normally, she wasn't afraid of heights, but the thought of crashing to the valley below made her feel sick to her stomach. She was cold and sweating at the same time.

"I'm right here." The fireman's eyes were kind as he leaned toward her. "I don't want to put any pressure on the tree branches holding you up, so I need you to take my hand."

She didn't want him to put any pressure on the tree branches holding her up either. The fireman's outstretched hand was well within reach. Darby forced her fingers to let go of the branch to grab him.

When his fingers locked strongly around hers, she nearly wept with relief. From there, she was able to let go and take his other hand, allowing him to pull her toward him. Some of the branches gave way, but suddenly she was up and inside the bucket with the firefighter.

Safe.

Darby managed to thank him as they were lowered to the ground. The kind fireman helped her out of the bucket, and for a moment, her knees threatened to buckle.

"The ambulance is this way." The fireman put a hand beneath her elbow, intending to escort her to where the EMTs waited.

She instinctively dug in her heels. "I'm fine, just bruised and sore." Her entire body ached, but she ignored it. Frankly, going through withdrawal six years ago had been far worse than this. "No broken bones, see?" She held out her arms and waved them up and down.

"They'll need to check you over anyway," the fireman insisted. "You can refuse to go to the hospital by signing a waiver."

A waiver, much like the one their guests signed to participate in zip lining. The irony was not lost on her. Darby removed her helmet and headed over to the EMTs. She endured their exam, then signed the waiver indicating she chose not to be transported to the hospital.

"Darby, what happened up there?" Kent demanded.

She handed him the helmet and the rest of her gear. "I

was going to ask you the same thing. Teddy thinks the zip line cable was tampered with."

Kent flushed with anger. "Who would do something crazy like that?"

"I don't know, Kent. Certainly not me. Maybe you should have the experts come and examine it to find out what happened?"

Kent paled. "You think I need to call the police?"

"I think this needs to be investigated, yes. By the police and the experts." She glanced down at her scratched and bleeding arms and legs. Thankfully, her injuries weren't severe. "If you don't mind, I need to clean up." She moved to brush past him, but he lifted a hand to stop her.

"I'm glad you're okay. Take the day off, Darby." His voice was softer now. "We'll get to the bottom of what happened here."

She nodded and walked past him. The zip lines would be closed for the rest of the day, and maybe even the rest of the week. Today was Monday, how long would it take to repair the cable? Or would they simply close that particular zip line down?

Darby hated to admit it, but she wasn't keen on the thought of going back up.

As she walked back to her car, she saw a tall muscular man with dark hair standing there. Her steps slowed as she recognized him.

Gage Killion.

No, it couldn't be. Not after all this time.

A shiver of apprehension snaked down her spine. What was Gage doing here? She hadn't seen him since she'd betrayed him, giving his name to the police in exchange for a stint in rehab rather than being sent to jail.

A decision that still haunted her all these years later.

"Darby." Gage didn't smile, his green eyes serious. "I saw what happened. Are you all right?"

"You saw?" She remembered the figure she'd glimpsed walking down below and felt a rush of anger. "Did you tamper with the cable as a way to get back at me?"

"No."

She folded her arms over her chest, lifting her chin and meeting his gaze head-on. "I don't believe you. It can't be a coincidence that you show up here to find me at the same time a cable breaks away, sending me crashing into a tree. I can hardly believe I'm walking away from that with just scratches and bruises to show for it."

"I did not tamper with the cable," he said firmly. "But I would like to talk to you. If you have time."

Time? She choked and swallowed a hysterical laugh. No way was she making time for Gage Killion.

The last thing she wanted was for Gage to discover he had a son.

WATCHING Darby swinging through the air as the cable gave way had shaved ten years off Gage's life. His palms were still damp with sweat from fear. It was easy to understand her suspicion, his timing couldn't have been worse.

Or maybe it was perfect timing. While she was being rescued, he'd hovered near the firetruck, melting in with the other adventure park visitors, and had heard a young kid mention the cable must have been tampered with.

He'd gone hot and cold in a nanosecond.

Had Tyrone Reyes beat him here?

"Please move away from my car." Darby stared at him as if he had a third eye. "I have to go."

"Thirty minutes." These days, he wasn't much of a conversationalist. Being locked up in jail for four years, he'd kept to himself as much as possible. Attending Bible study sessions had become his salvation, but even then he hadn't done much talking, spending most of his time listening and soaking up the knowledge.

It had been strange how much talking he'd been forced to do since being released. He took a half step toward her. "Please."

Darby looked away, and he could tell she wasn't the least bit interested in talking to him.

"It's important," he urged. "I think I know who tampered with that cable."

She spun back to face him, her gray eyes wide. She wore her straight blonde hair shorter now, chin length rather than down to the middle of her back. The shorter length suited her. She looked beautiful and healthy. He was extremely relieved there was no sign of her being a drug user.

"Thirty minutes," she reluctantly agreed. "There's a coffee shop down the road. We'll walk."

"Okay." He was hardly in a position to argue. Darby gave him a wide berth, as if the idea of touching him, even in passing, was abhorrent. She headed down the blacktop driveway to the Keystone Coffee Café.

"How and why did you find me?"

Darby's abrupt question caught him off guard. He didn't want to come across as some sort of stalker, but then again, he'd called in a few favors to find her. "It's a long story."

She let out a snort, calling him on his lie. Well, not a lie exactly, but a half truth. This wasn't the time to get into all of that now, though. She'd only agreed to thirty minutes, and walking to the coffee shop had taken up a few of them.

They entered the coffee shop and found a table near the window.

"Do you still take cream and sugar?" He gestured to the cashier. "I'm buying."

"Yes." She didn't thank him and still looked as if she might jump up and run the moment his back was turned.

He hoped and prayed she wouldn't.

After buying two coffees, he returned to the table. Darby took hers hesitantly as if he might have poisoned it. The way she'd accused him of breaking her cable stung. She clearly didn't trust him in any way, shape, or form.

"Why are you here?" Darby didn't beat around the bush. She took a sip of her doctored coffee, eyeing him over the rim.

He decided to get straight to the point. "Tyrone Reyes is out of jail."

Her hand jerked, spilling some of her coffee. "Recently?"

"Within the past thirty days. You know as well as I do he's the type to seek revenge."

She stared down at her cup for a long moment before looking up at him. "He knows—everything?"

Gage knew what she was really asking. "He knows you gave me up to the police, and through me, got to him. So yeah, he knows everything."

Darby drew in a deep breath, then said very quietly, "I did what I had to do."

"I know." He couldn't lie and say it hadn't hurt. Yet at the same time, he'd understood she'd been forced to look out for herself. Honestly, wasn't that the reason he'd rolled on Reyes? It was the way the legal system worked. Small-time drug dealers like him were only snagged to get to the bigger fish. There was no such thing as honor among thieves.

Gage wasn't proud of what he'd done. He'd escaped one abusive situation only to find himself in a worse position. He'd admit he made poor choices and lived to regret them. He still thought of those months as the dark years, and he was determined to never, ever go back. But the months he'd spent with Darby weren't all bad. In fact, she was the one and only bright spot in his mind.

Too bad she didn't feel the same way about him.

"You really think Reyes damaged the zip line cable in an attempt to hurt me?"

Darby's question pulled him from his thoughts. "I don't know. I didn't see him anywhere nearby, but he might have hired someone to do the dirty work for him. You're the one who mentioned the strange coincidence."

She lifted her gray eyes to his, and he saw a hint of defiance intermixed with fear. "Give me one good reason why I should believe you? You could have damaged the cable yourself, only to pin the deed on Tyrone Reyes." She hesitated, then added, "And you have a reason to get back at me, more than he does."

"I would never hurt you, Darby. And I don't blame you for what happened."

Darby let out a harsh laugh. "Yeah, right. How many years of jail time did you do because of me? Three?"

Four, with two years' probation, but who was counting? "I mean it." He leaned forward, trying to get her to understand. "I don't blame you for ratting me out. It's each man or woman for themselves at a time like that. Besides, who do you think rolled on Reyes?"

She looked away. "I did. Although all I really knew was his name and that he pretty much made the drug deals that you carried out on his behalf."

"Yeah, well after they arrested me, I blabbed about

everything. I gave them details about Reyes and each of the drug dealers working for him, and lots of other information you couldn't possibly know, Darby. And it worked, Reyes was busted right after me. In fact, I'm not sure how he managed to get out of the joint with a sentence of only five and a half years, unless he turned around and made the same deal."

Her gray eyes widened, and her voice dropped to a whisper. "You think Reyes turned on someone higher up in the organization?"

"Yeah, I do. But being forced to do that probably only made Reyes even more angry. The entire network had to have fallen to pieces by the series of arrests." Something he didn't feel the least bit sorry about. He hadn't gotten addicted to the stuff the way Darby had, but he'd stayed sober since being set free. And he had no intention of being involved in anything criminal ever again. "I firmly believe Reyes will come after me. In fact, I think he was responsible for my car being run off the road this past weekend." He'd suspected it wasn't an accident, but after watching Darby crash into a tree, he knew for sure it wasn't.

A flash of concern darkened her gaze. "You weren't hurt?"

"I'm fine." He waved a hand. "But if Reyes is responsible for the cable malfunction, he's definitely upped his game. The car collision wasn't nearly as serious as what you just experienced. I'm worried he'll keep on trying until he's succeeded in hurting us, or worse."

Darby abruptly jumped up from her seat. "I have to go."

"Wait, shouldn't we . . ." but he was talking to the air as Darby had already bolted from the coffee shop, the door slamming shut with a loud bang behind her.

CHAPTER TWO

Leo, Leo, Leo.

Darby repeated her son's name in her mind as she sprinted to her car, an old Honda Accord with well over a hundred thousand miles on it. If Gage was right about Tyrone coming after them, she needed to protect her son.

Their son.

No, she shook her head as she drove to the side-by-side townhouse. Gage might look more muscular and handsome than he had before, but that didn't mean he wasn't planning to go back to his old ways. Even if he intended to go straight, she wasn't about to confuse her son by introducing a father who may either leave the area or end up back in jail.

She could only control her own actions. Her own vow to maintain sobriety. She didn't have enough time or energy to waste on Gage.

Pulling into the driveway of their side of the building, Darby jumped out and ran up to the door. It was locked, so she used her key to gain access.

"Edith? Leo?" Her voice bounced off the walls. It took

her a minute to realize they weren't home and belatedly remembered Edith's plan to take Leo to the park.

What if they were followed there by Reyes or his men? She spun around and ran back out to her car. The park wasn't far, Edith preferred to walk with Leo, but Darby wasn't about to waste another second.

She desperately needed to know that Edith and Leo were both safe.

The park was full of people enjoying the sunny June day. The parking lot was packed, but she eventually found a spot. Realizing it would be impossible to find Edith and Leo amidst the crowds, she called Edith's cell phone.

"Hi, Darby, are you on break already?" Edith asked.

The sound of Edith's sweet voice provided the sense of calm she desperately needed. "Not exactly, I'm at the park. Where are you and Leo?"

"Leo is playing on the swing. But I don't understand, why aren't you at work?" A hint of worry crept into Edith's voice. Darby knew she was likely imagining the worst. That Darby may have succumbed to temptation, falling back into the dark abyss of drug addiction.

Sweeping her gaze over the park, she spotted the swing set and noted Leo was being pushed on one of the swings by Edith. "I see you. I'll explain soon." Without saying anything more, Darby disconnected and jogged over to the swings. Just seeing Leo giggling as he was pushed higher and higher made her smile in relief.

They were fine.

"Mommy!" Leo jumped off the swing and rushed over to hug her. She swept the boy into her arms, inhaling the scent of grass and baby shampoo and closing her eyes in gratitude that he was okay.

"Hey, kiddo." She had to blink wetness from her eyes. "Looks like you were having fun."

"I love swinging." As quickly as he'd hugged her, he broke away from their embrace to return to his swing. Edith obliged by pushing him again.

"Goodness, Darby, what on earth happened to you?"

Edith's exclamation confused her for a moment before she remembered her scratched and bleeding arms and legs. "Oh, yeah." She stared down at herself for a moment, wishing she'd taken a shower first before charging over. But paralyzing fear had overwhelmed all logical thought. "Uh, there was an accident, so I was sent home for the day."

"What kind of accident?" Edith's warm brown eyes widened with horror. "Not on the zip line?"

"Yes, but look, I'm fine. Just a few scrapes and bruises." Darby didn't go into detail about how the fire department had rescued her. No point in worrying Edith any more than she was already. Only now that she was at the park, Darby wasn't sure how to proceed. "Edith, have you noticed anything unusual? A stranger hanging around? Anything out of the ordinary?"

"No, why?" Edith's gaze sharpened. "Are you worried about Leo's father?"

That Edith had gone there surprised her. Darby hadn't given the woman many details about Gage, other than to say he was in jail. To be honest, Darby hadn't wanted to admit that she was the one who'd betrayed him, resulting in his arrest.

Interesting that Gage hadn't blamed her for ratting him out but had in fact turned around to give evidence against Tyrone Reyes. She wasn't sure what to make of that, but she reminded herself it didn't matter. Gage had come to warn her, which was nice. But she had no intention of getting personally involved with him.

Frankly, she'd never imagined she'd see him again.

"Not really." Darby sighed, realizing she hadn't thought this through. How much about all of this should she share? Leo's safety was a top priority, Edith's too. But that would mean explaining about the cable being tampered with and the details about why Reyes might be seeking revenge.

"Darby, what's wrong?" Edith's tone was full of concern. "You look upset."

"I, uh, the accident may have rattled me more than I realized." She hated to cut Leo's time in the park short, but discussing the danger in the midst of a crowd wasn't optimal. Darby glanced around but didn't see anyone lurking nearby. "How long do you and Leo usually hang out?"

"We usually head back for lunch." Edith eyed her thoughtfully. "What is it you're not telling me?"

A smile tugged at the corner of her mouth. She never could put anything past Edith. She was sharp and knew Darby better than she knew herself. "I'll explain when we get home."

"Okay." To her credit, Edith didn't push for more.

Darby took over pushing her son on the swing, enjoying the sound of his laughter. When Leo was tired of that, he ran over to the slide. Watching him play made her thoughts return to Gage.

He shouldn't have looked so good. She was only eighteen when they'd gotten together. Despite the drug dealing and her own addiction, they'd had some good times together. Which probably sounded strange to people who hadn't lived as they had.

Darby's previous boyfriend, Aaron, had turned abusive. She'd taken off with him after a fight with Hailey. A stupid move that Darby had later regretted. But then she'd met Gage, who was also part of the drug community. He'd always been sweet and nice, despite his determination to make money selling drugs. They'd both suffered abuse growing up, something that had drawn them together. Probably not in a healthy way.

Gage was her past, something she'd locked away in her quest to move forward in providing Leo the love and stability he deserved. Having Gage show up out of the blue had seriously knocked her off balance. He was a threat to her newfound equilibrium.

After an hour of playing, Leo complained of being hungry. Since she had her car, along with Leo's car seat, she drove them back to the townhouse.

"I planned to make grilled cheese sandwiches for lunch, unless you'd like something different?" Edith asked. "I have a roast in the Crock-Pot for dinner."

Edith's mother was born in Germany, immigrating here when she was young. Edith loved using her mother's recipes, which tended to be heavy on the meat and potatoes. For years, Darby hadn't known where her next meal was coming from, so she ate whatever Edith prepared without complaint.

"Sounds perfect to me." She was already planning to set up a movie for Leo when lunch was finished so she could speak privately to Edith about the threat of danger.

Maybe even convince Edith to take Leo away for a few days. The thought of not seeing her son every day, tucking him into bed every night, made her heart ache, but she'd do whatever was necessary to keep him safe.

She pulled into the driveway. As she was unbuckling Leo from his car seat—he was small for his age, so he hadn't graduated yet to the booster seat—she heard her name.

"Hi, Darby."

She startled so badly she almost dropped her son. Turning, she glared at Gage. What on earth was he doing here? Had he followed her? Was he stalking her? Could the whole story about Tyrone Reyes be a big fat lie?

"How did you find me?" Her harsh tone garnered an alarming look from Edith.

Gage held up a hand. "I just want to talk. You didn't give me my full thirty minutes." His green eyes landed on Leo.

"Leo, go inside with your oma, okay?" She practically thrust the child at Edith. "I'll be in soon."

Edith eyed Gage curiously as she took Leo's hand. Her son must have been hungry because he didn't ask about Gage.

"Yours?" Gage asked.

She did not want to have this conversation. "Edith's grandson." Yeah, it was a bit of a lie, but a necessary one until she knew she could trust this man who kept showing up wherever she was. First her place of work, now her home. "And you didn't answer my question, how did you find me?"

"I learned your address from that kid you work with," he admitted. "But I only came because of the danger Reyes presents to us."

"Sure." She snorted and glared at him as she pulled out her phone. "I'm this close to calling the police. Stalking is a crime, and I don't appreciate you popping up without warning."

"It's not like I have your phone number," Gage countered. "I can't stop you from calling the police, Darby. But I promise I'm not here to hurt you." He hesitated, then added, "Or your son."

She sucked in a harsh breath, wondering how he'd guessed. Leo did have her same blond hair, and they shared the same nose, but his eyes were green.

The same shade as Gage's.

"Are you married now?" Gage asked.

She frowned, then understood he'd assumed she was still with Leo's father. For a moment she wavered, feeling guilty for keeping her son's parentage a secret. "No. I've never been married. You?"

"No one is interested in marrying a former convict," Gage said dryly. "Look, Darby, I really think we need to work together on this."

"Work together on what?" She wasn't following his train of thought. "There's nothing for us to do, Gage. Other than to notify the police."

"We should do that," he agreed. "But if Reyes is trying to hurt us, we need to stick together. Maybe catch him or his associate in the act. It's always better to go on offense than to sit around and wait for the next strike."

Darby didn't want to admit she hadn't thought that far ahead. First, she needed to get Edith and Leo out of town for a while. Then she could think about the rest.

Joining forces with Gabe had never crossed her mind.

But there was something to be said for going on offense. "I'll think about it."

A flash of disappointment crossed his features, and she couldn't help wondering if he'd expected her to invite him in. Yeah, so not happening. "Okay, could I get your phone number? That way I can call you rather than showing up without warning."

It was a reasonable request. She held up her phone. "Give me your number."

He recited the information, and she added him to her

contact list. Then she called him so he could get her number.

"Thanks." He hesitated, then added, "I'm staying in a motel in town, just two miles from the adventure park. If you have time later, I'd like to meet for dinner, say around six o'clock? We can create a game plan then."

Dinner? It sounded suspiciously like a date. Something she hadn't had in the six years she'd been sober. Not because she hadn't been asked out, but simply because she wasn't interested. Especially since most men wanted to meet after work for a drink, something she wasn't going to do.

"Please?" Gage pressed.

"Okay, dinner at six. Maybe at the Red Mill?" She named the family-style restaurant she'd taken Leo to on occasion. Her experience only extended to kid-friendly restaurants, so if Gage was expecting something more, he'd be sorely disappointed.

"That would be great. Thanks, Darby." Gage gave her a nod and walked away. She noticed he got behind the wheel of a battered white pickup truck parked down the road.

A truck she hadn't noticed. Which didn't say much for her keen observation skills.

She watched for a moment as he drove off, wondering if meeting him for dinner was a mistake she'd come to regret.

In more ways than one.

LEARNING Darby had a son surprised him. The kid was cute, no question about it, and he'd instantly seen Darby's features on the boy's face. Which made him wonder about the boy's father.

Considering he hadn't seen Darby in six years, it made sense she'd gotten involved with another man. And even though she claimed she wasn't married, he figured the guy must be making child support payments.

He told himself Darby's love life was none of his business. Just because he still found her incredibly attractive, more so than when she'd been addicted to painkillers, didn't mean she felt the same way.

In fact, he was getting the sense she didn't like him at all. The revelation shouldn't have hurt, but it did. And really, he couldn't blame her. He likely represented a time in her life she'd sooner forget.

Gage drove back to his low-budget motel, keeping a wary eye on the vehicles behind him. He hadn't been prepared for the rear-end collision that had sent him spinning out of control outside of Knoxville. The only good news around the event was that his truck hadn't sustained much damage, other than a crushed rear bumper, and no one else had been hurt either. He'd known God was watching over him as he'd managed to stay on the road.

The black SUV that had hit him had taken off, and while the police arrived to investigate, no one had gotten the license plate number.

There was no sign of a black SUV following him now. Still, he couldn't ignore the possibility that Reyes or his associates were out there, watching him.

At least he knew now why Darby had bolted from the coffee shop. She must have worried that her son was in danger. Knowing she had a young boy complicated things. As if they weren't complicated enough already.

After taking a detoured path to his motel, he pulled into the lot and parked several doors away from his own room. He swept a gaze over the parking lot, but he didn't see anything suspicious. Being a reformed criminal had honed his observation skills. Back then, he'd always been on the lookout for a cop, but now he searched for a sign of Reyes or one of his men.

Thankfully, everything looked fine. Using the key, he unlocked his door. The scent of mold and mildew hit hard when he went inside, but he forced himself to ignore it. The place was cheap, which was all that mattered.

After being released from jail, he'd been blessed to land a job with a construction company. His boss had granted him only one week off and fully expected Gage to report back to work by next Monday. Gage didn't want to lose his position, the hard physical labor beneath the hot Tennessee sun had been a lifeline over the past forty-eight months after spending four years in a jail cell.

Ironic that Darby had also found a job working outside. He'd been impressed when he'd heard her giving the group of attendees a safety lecture. Thinking again of her near-death experience on the zip line made him frown.

The police would surely investigate. And if they deemed the zip line cable had been tampered with, they'd take his and Darby's concerns around Tyrone Reyes more seriously.

At least, they should. Unfortunately, Gage had found that his criminal record worked against him at times like this. The cop who'd responded to the scene of the rear-end collision had not seemed inclined to believe the crash had been done on purpose. His being on probation, set to end in the next three months, probably hadn't helped.

He hoped and prayed they'd believe Darby. Although she had a conviction for drugs on her record too.

Sitting around and doing nothing wasn't his style, so Gage decided to head out to grab something to eat. He also wanted to find the restaurant Darby mentioned. His construction company was located on the other side of Knoxville, and that's where he'd spent most of his time since being released. His parole didn't require him to stay in a certain neighborhood as long as he didn't miss any of his now monthly check-ins.

Gage went on foot, thinking it would be easier to spot a tail that way.

Darby had asked how he'd found her. He'd called in a few favors from some of their former friends. Maggie, in particular, seemed to know the most, telling him Darby had gone into rehab and had gotten a job at the Great Outdoor Adventure Park. Checking out their website, he'd noticed Darby was in a staff photograph. Maggie claimed they were both clean, but he'd noticed the girl had been twitchy, so he wasn't convinced. Still, he'd risked consorting with known criminals to find Darby.

And he could admit now that his need to see her had stemmed from something more than just fear for her safety.

He'd thought about Darby a lot over the past few years. More so since he'd been released from prison. He was glad he'd been able to talk to her about what had transpired back then. It was important that she understood that he didn't blame her for giving him up to the cops.

Looking back, Gage knew that going to prison had saved his life. He'd been spiraling down a dark and dangerous path. Hurting people by dealing drugs to them, making himself a target for other drug dealers who could steal from him. It shamed him now, but he'd worked hard over the years to learn how to forgive himself for those mistakes.

Learning about God's forgiveness had helped. The pastor who taught Bible study in prison had been equally encouraging, stressing to Gage that focusing on the future was far better than remaining mired in the past.

Had Darby learned that lesson too? He hoped so.

Gage grabbed a burger from a fast-food restaurant, walking as he ate. Out of the corner of his eye he caught a glimpse of a man blatantly staring at him. With as much nonchalance as he could muster, he turned toward the guy to get a better look, bringing his sandwich up to help cover his face.

The man smiled and waved. He felt foolish as he belatedly realized there was a woman standing behind him.

Yeah, he needed to stop being paranoid. If Tyrone really wanted to extract his pound of flesh, Gage doubted the guy would come after him in broad daylight. Gage had to assume whatever tampering that had impacted the zip line cable had been done earlier that morning when there was no one around to see.

The rest of the day passed with agonizing slowness. At five fifteen, he showered and changed into clean clothes. It was ridiculous how much he wanted to look nice for Darby, considering she'd made her feelings toward him abundantly clear.

He swallowed his nervousness as he walked to the Red Mill Family-Style Restaurant. Darby came in as he waited for the hostess to return to the station.

"Hi, you look amazing." The words popped out of his mouth before he could think about it, but they were true. Her hair fell soft and silky to her chin, and she wore a yellow blouse with blue jeans, which should have been casual but made her look stunning.

She didn't smile, her gaze wary. "You look nice too. I guess we've both come a long way since the last time we saw each other."

He was surprised she'd brought up the past. "Yes, we have." He turned his attention to the hostess. "Table for two please?"

"This way."

When they were seated at a small table in a corner of the restaurant, they took a minute to scan the menu. The menu had a variety of options, including a nice kid's meal section, and was reasonably priced. Now that he'd seen her son, he understood why she'd chosen the place. Once their server took their orders, he leaned forward. "Have you learned anything more on the cable incident?"

Darby grimaced. "My boss called to let me know the police are still investigating. They haven't decided if the cable broke by accident or had help."

"Did you give a statement to the police?"

She slowly shook her head. "After the firemen brought me down, they had the EMTs look at me, then told me I was free to leave. I haven't been contacted since." She hesitated, then added, "How are we ever going to prove Tyrone Reyes is involved when we can't even say for sure the cable was tampered with?"

"I know, it's the same problem I had," he confessed, taking a sip of his water. "The cop who responded to the scene of the accident told me that there was no proof that the rear-end collision had been done on purpose."

Darby frowned. "Do you think this is all part of Reyes's plan? To attempt to cause us harm without making it appear like a personal vendetta?"

"It's worked so far, hasn't it?" He sighed. "And what about your son? I'm concerned he could be in danger too."

Darby straightened and reached for her water glass. "I never said he was my son."

"Come on, Darby. The kid is a spitting image of you."

Gage eyed her across the table. "I hope you're getting child support."

She began to cough, the water she'd sipped going down the wrong pipe. She pressed her napkin to her face as she tried to get her coughing fit under control.

"Are you okay?" he asked.

"Fine." Her voice sounded hoarse. "Sorry, we were discussing Reyes and what, if anything, we can do to find him."

No, they'd been discussing her son, but he decided to drop the subject. At least for now. "I think we need to consider hiring a private investigator."

She gaped at him. "Seriously? I mean, it would be nice, but I don't have that kind of money. The park doesn't pay that well, I'm just making enough to get by."

He wanted to ask again about child support but thought better of it. "I have a job with a construction company, and business has skyrocketed, so I can pay the fee." It wouldn't be easy since his credit rating was terrible due to his stint in prison, but it would be worth the sacrifice. "Do you have a better idea?"

She grimaced. "No. Other than trying to find him ourselves."

"I have the rest of the week off," he admitted. "I can try to poke around a bit before I have to return to work."

"My boss told me to stay home tomorrow since the zip line has been shut down." Darby spread her hands. "But where do we even start? We can't even say for sure Reyes is the one doing this. As you pointed out, he could have paid someone."

Their meals arrived, and they ate for a bit in silence. He wanted to bring the subject back around to her son, but it was clearly a touchy topic.

"Maybe we meet tomorrow at the police station. I think you need to let them know that Reyes may have tampered with the zip line cable." He waited a bit, then added, "And you need to think of a way to protect your son."

She nodded. "I've asked Edith to take Leo away for a few days."

"Smart move."

There was another long pause before she said, "There's something you should know. Leo turned five last month."

Five? He assumed the kid was younger. Then the math hit him. "Mine? Are you telling me Leo is my son?" The idea was staggering. No wonder she'd choked when he'd mentioned child support.

She lifted her chin. "Yes. But don't think you're going to be a part of his life, Gage, because he and Edith have already left town. I'm only telling you because if Reyes is coming after us, I want you to be aware that he may use Leo as a pawn. Against both of us."

The initial flash of anger he'd felt at her deception faded. Because she was right. If Reyes ever found out about Leo, the child would be a target.

And Gage absolutely refused to allow that to happen.

CHAPTER THREE

Darby had debated with herself all afternoon about whether or not to tell Gage the truth about Leo. She would have kept the revelation a secret, but the nagging possibility of Reyes coming after them had broken through her resolve.

Selfishly, she hadn't wanted to share Leo with Gage. Yet, in the end, Leo needed to stay safe, no matter how she felt about the situation. It was a no-brainer decision to tell Gage the truth in order to protect her son.

Their son.

A lump of emotion lodged in her throat. Never had she imagined meeting up with Gage and telling him about Leo. At some point down the line, Darby knew she'd probably regret this. But she'd have bigger regrets if she remained silent and something bad happened to the innocent little boy.

She'd made the decision to keep him. She needed to make the right decision now to protect him.

"I can't believe you didn't tell me you were pregnant."

Gage's hoarse voice broke into her thoughts. She met his gaze straight on, not the least bit apologetic. "Why? I betrayed you by sending you to jail. I didn't think you'd welcome the news. Or be in any position to do anything about it." At the time, she'd been secretly glad Gage had been in jail. It had made it easy to keep the news of her pregnancy to herself.

"He's the reason you made that deal with the DA's office." It was a statement, not a question.

She lifted her chin. "I knew I needed to get clean for the sake of the baby. So yeah, I made the decision to turn you in to the police so that I would be placed in rehab rather than sent to jail. And once I beat the addiction, I made the decision to keep my baby." The first few weeks had been extremely difficult but worth the agony in the long run. After three months, Darby had been moved from rehab to the halfway house. Most of the staff there urged her to give Leo up for adoption. An option she had seriously considered. But, deep down, she'd suspected that going down that path would be detrimental to her emotional well-being. Leo gave her a reason to stay clean. To work hard and to provide him the life he deserved.

Without having him as an anchor, she'd have caved to the temptation of returning to her old ways. Thankfully, Edith had befriended her at the halfway house, sharing the story about her daughter's death from an overdose. Darby knew then and there she could very easily end up the same way.

Six years sober. It was a milestone, and one she didn't take lightly.

"Okay, I can grant you that, but what about when we first met earlier today? Once you knew I was out of jail? Or when I came to your townhouse? Why didn't you say something sooner?" Gage persisted. "You lied and told me that Leo was that woman's grandson."

"It's not a lie, Edith is Leo's grandmother in every way that counts. And I didn't say anything about you being his father because I didn't trust you." He winced, and she felt a weird pang of regret at hurting him. But then she pushed on. "You're losing sight of what is important here, Gage. I'm telling you the truth now because Leo could be in danger. We need to figure out how to ensure his safety."

He sat back and let out a heavy sigh. "You're right, we do need to ensure Leo's safety. Cut me a little slack, Darby. It's not every day you learn you're a father. Oh, and just so you know? I will absolutely be a part of my son's life."

The words caused a pang in the region of her heart. From this point on, her life would be irrevocably changed. She'd known Gage wouldn't settle for anything less than having a relationship with his son.

She wrestled back a surge of panic. There would be time to worry about that later. Right now, they needed to remain focused on Tyrone Reyes. "What time?"

Gage blinked in confusion. For the past five years, she'd thought of Gage every time she looked into Leo's green eyes. "What time what?"

"You said we start tomorrow by going to the police department. What time?"

His expression cleared. "Eight thirty. But let's go back a minute. You mentioned sending Edith and Leo off somewhere. How long will they be gone? And does that mean you'll be all alone in the townhouse?"

Wary of where he was going, she straightened in her seat. "They'll be gone the rest of this week. I'm hoping they'll be able to return on the weekend. And whether I live alone is none of your business. I'm not interested in picking up where we left off six years ago."

Again, a flash of hurt crossed his face. "I never expected

that, Darby. My only concern is for your safety. Being alone in the townhouse isn't smart. Who's to say that you weren't followed at some point?"

She flushed, realizing she shouldn't have gone down that path of assuming he wanted something more from her. And probably wouldn't have if she didn't still find Gage attractive. "I'll be fine."

He shot her an exasperated look. "Don't minimize the danger, Darby. It's only a matter of time until Reyes strikes again."

A ripple of fear skated down her spine, and she had to resist the urge to look over her shoulder. Ridiculous as they were in a crowded restaurant. No way would Reyes try something in front of this many witnesses. Although wasn't that the point Gage was making?

If by some chance Reyes knew where she lived, staying there alone would make her vulnerable. If the cable was cut intentionally, the person who'd done the deed had not only known she worked there but also knew her routine. That she always went across the zip line first, before any of the guests.

"I was thinking it might be smart for you to stay at the same motel I'm in," Gage continued. "At least for tonight, until we find out from the police if they're willing to take the potential threat against you seriously."

"Against us," she clarified. It would take a chunk of money, but she decided to do as he suggested. "Okay, I'll stay there for tonight. But I need to head home long enough to pack a few things."

Gage frowned. "I'll go with you."

She reluctantly nodded. He'd scared her enough that being with him was better than wandering around the area alone. "Thanks."

Darby's appetite had vanished, but she finished her meal anyway. Years of never knowing when to expect food had programmed her to never leave food on her plate. She'd taken more than one box of leftovers home, always grateful to get two meals out of one.

Watching Gage eat, she realized he shared the same mentality. Their abusive pasts had drawn them together seven years ago. But she hadn't told him everything about life with the Preacher.

Using drugs had been her pathetic attempt to forget all about it.

She glanced up as their server approached with their bill. Gage took it and fished for his wallet.

"I can pay my share." She didn't normally carry a lot of cash and made a mental note to stop at the closest cash machine.

"I invited you," Gage reminded her. "And it's the least I can do since I haven't paid a dime of child support in the past five years."

"It's not like you could have paid anything from jail," she shot back, then winced. "I'm sorry, that was rude."

"Yes, it was." Gage stood. "But it's also true. Come on, the motel isn't far."

Darby told herself to get a grip as she followed him from the restaurant. Being with Gage again, all these years later, felt strange. Not only were they both sober and productive members of society, but they shared a bond that could never be broken.

Leo.

Ignoring her innate attraction to him was proving to be more difficult than she'd anticipated. Still, she did her best to maintain her distance, stopping near her car. "It's better if I drive, don't you think?"

Gage turned and looked as if he might argue. But then he nodded and retraced his steps to join her. "Sure, that works."

The drive to her townhouse didn't take long, but a heavy silence hung between them as if they were both lost in their own thoughts.

"How long have you lived here?" Gage's question came as she pulled into the driveway.

"About eighteen months. Before that, we lived together in a small apartment."

"All three of you?" His tone rose in surprise.

"Yes." A ghost of a smile crossed her features. "I think Edith was testing me out, making sure I had the strength and determination to stay clean."

"She sounds like an amazing woman." Gage slid out from the passenger seat.

"She is all that and more." Pulling out her keys, she glanced at him. "I wouldn't have been able to raise Leo and work without her help."

"I'm glad God was watching over you and Leo," Gage said softly.

"God?" She let out a harsh laugh as she unlocked the door. "I don't believe that for a second."

"I'm sorry to hear that." Gage followed her inside. "Learning about God and his teachings through the Bible is what got me through four years of prison. I've come a long way since the last time we saw each other."

The news surprised her, but she decided to let the subject drop. Gage didn't know how the Preacher had screamed at her and her foster siblings, beating them with switches as he railed about how they were all sinners who God needed to punish. Just the memory of those beatings made her sick to her stomach. The night they'd managed to escape, thanks especially to Hailey, Sawyer, and Jayme, she'd been relieved and thankful for the ability to start a new life.

Hailey had taken her under her wing and had introduced her as a younger sister. But they'd soon learned that living on the street was no picnic. Better than being in the cellar of the Preacher's cabin, but not by much. Even with Hailey's help, they went hungry more often than not.

And the nightmares of those years with the Preacher and Ruth had held her back, making it difficult to move forward.

Especially the role she'd played in what had happened that night.

GAGE KNEW he'd hit yet another sore spot with his comments about God. Darby had ignored him, disappearing into her room without saying a word.

With a sigh, he took a moment to scan his surroundings. The townhouse Darby and Leo called home was nice and spacious, bigger than the efficiency apartment he lived in. Although he could understand why she'd want something like this for Leo.

Leo. He was still grappling with the news that he had a child. A son. He wished now that he'd taken the time to look at the little boy more closely. To initiate a conversation with him. To Gage's chagrin, it hadn't crossed his mind that he might be the kid's father.

Even though it should have. He and Darby had been together, intimately, for over a year.

But knowing the truth put everything that had happened six years ago into perspective. As upset as he was at uncovering Darby's secret, he was proud of the difficult decision she'd made.

She'd chosen to get clean for the baby's sake. Turning him in so that she could enter rehab. And she'd stayed clean all these years later. He'd heard of some drug abuse success stories, but not many. More often than not users went back to their old ways.

But Darby had pulled herself together, creating a nice life for herself and their son. He knew she could have easily given the baby up for adoption. And if she had, he'd never know his son even existed.

He was fiercely glad Darby had found Edith. The fact that the woman had taken Leo away for the rest of the week told him that she was extremely loyal to Darby.

He had no doubt that Edith would keep Leo safe.

On the heels of that thought came another. Edith would keep Leo safe, but her actions would be hampered by the fact that she didn't know what Tyrone Reyes looked like. If Reyes was the one doing the dirty work.

He began to pace the length of the living room. They needed to get a copy of Reyes's mug shot to Edith so she could be on the lookout for the guy. And if Reyes had hired a stranger to run him off the road and to tamper with the zip line? He winced and realized there was nothing they could do about that.

He and Darby would be equally hampered by that scenario.

"I'm ready to go." Darby emerged from the bedroom carrying a small duffel bag. She'd changed out of the blouse and into a plain T-shirt.

"Great." He met her halfway, taking the bag from her fingers. "I was thinking it would be a good idea to get Edith a copy of Tyrone's mug shot. It would be helpful for her to be on the lookout for him."

She blanched and nodded. "That's a good idea. I personally have never seen the guy, so it would be good for me too."

"You don't happen to have a computer, do you?" A quick glance didn't reveal any such device.

"No. I use the library if I need computer access." She moved past him to the door. "But we might want to make that another stop tomorrow so I can text a copy to Edith."

"Yeah." He followed her out of the townhouse. "What's Edith's last name?"

She frowned as she locked the door. "Why do you want to know?"

"I'm just curious. She seems almost too good to be true."

That got Darby's back up. "She's a wonderful woman who lost her own daughter to a drug overdose. She was a volunteer at the halfway house and super supportive of me and Leo."

He lifted a hand in protest. "I didn't mean to insinuate she wasn't a good person, Darby. I just wondered why she was living with you and Leo, that's all."

She relaxed and led the way back to the car. "It's more like me and Leo are living with her. At least, that's how it was at first. Now it's more of a partnership. We split the rent, she uses the social security money from her deceased husband. I pay the grocery bills and pay for Leo's clothes and preschool while she pays the utilities. We don't lead a lavish lifestyle as you can see. We don't even have cable TV, although I'm already hearing about that from Leo as his preschool friends all do."

"I'm very glad you and Leo have Edith," he said sincerely.

"Me too." Darby slid behind the wheel.

After storing her duffel in the back, he settled into the passenger seat. "We could swing by the library tonight. I would think it's still open."

She shot him a glance, then nodded. "Okay. And her last name is Schroeder."

"German?" he guessed.

"Yes. That's why she's asked Leo to call her Oma." She backed out of the driveway of the townhouse.

"I like that." He was deeply grateful to know his son had a woman he could love like a grandmother. His own mother had turned a blind eye to the physical abuse his stepfather was bestowing on him. Gage hadn't seen the woman since he'd left home at fifteen. By the time he'd tried to find her after prison, the place had been sold to a young couple with a new baby without any sign of where his mother and stepfather had gone. And he knew Darby had been in foster care, so it wasn't like there would be grandparents on her side either.

It bothered him to hear that Darby didn't believe in God, especially since he knew full well God had sent Edith to help her. But he wasn't about to disturb the fragile truce between them.

The most important thing right now was for them to work together to figure out if Reyes was the one behind these attacks. And to get the police to take the snapped cable at the adventure park that could have killed Darby seriously.

The trip to the library didn't take long. Ironically, it was located squarely between his studio apartment and Darby and Edith's townhouse. He was secretly amazed he and Darby hadn't run into each other there over the past year. Although he normally stopped in late, after a long day of work, whereas she probably went in with Leo on her days off.

Within minutes, they were huddled in front of a computer. "How do we find Reyes?" Darby whispered, her fingers hovering over the keyboard.

"Search on his name and add the word arrest and see what comes up."

Darby typed in Tyrone Reyes's name, and several links popped up. He tapped a finger over the link halfway down the page. "This looks like it's an article about his arrest."

She clicked the link. Sure enough, a reporter from the Knoxville News had written about Tyrone's arrest, including a picture of his mug shot. Darby manipulated the picture to make it larger, then pulled out her phone. After snapping a picture of the grainy photograph, she sent a text to Edith.

"Let's print this out," Gage suggested. "Might help to show the cops."

"There's a fee for printing, but I agree it's worth it." She punched the print key and then walked over to the desk to pay.

He continued looking at Reyes's face on the screen. It seemed to him that Reyes stared back at him with cold, dead eyes. A flash of regret hit hard. How had he allowed himself to get mixed up with Reyes in the first place? Yeah, he needed money to survive on the streets, but he was also old enough to know better than to get involved in selling drugs.

"Gage? Is there something more you think we should try to search? Any other names you think might be involved?"

"Huh? Oh, no. Not that I can think of offhand." He shoved the mistakes of his past aside. There was no point in dwelling on them.

Pastor Davies had convinced him that God had forgiven all of Gage's sins. Most of the time, he believed that to be true. But every so often the magnitude of what he'd done allowed the deep-seated doubts to creep in. He'd sold drugs, likely contributed to drug overdoses. Maybe even to deaths, like Edith's daughter.

With an effort, Gage turned his attention back to the computer. Other names? "Wait a minute, there is one other guy who I ratted out. Niles Archer." He worked the keyboard, bringing up Archer's arrest, which had taken place a few days after Reyes's. When Archer's mug shot bloomed on the screen, he gestured to it. "Does he look familiar to you?"

Darby studied the photograph. "He does," she admitted. "But I can't say for sure when I saw him. Not recently, but back when we were together."

A surge of adrenaline kicked his pulse into high gear. "Maybe Reyes and Archer are working together on this. They would both have a good reason to seek revenge. I wonder if Archer was released at the same time as Reyes hit the street." Archer didn't scare him as much as Reyes. "We need to print this article too. I can pay for it."

"I've got it. But let me snap a pic first." She blew up the image and used her phone again, taking the picture and texting it to Edith. Then she headed back to the desk to pay the fee.

With both articles in hand, Darby led the way out of the library and down to the parking lot where she'd left her car.

Gage felt good about having two potential suspects. Especially if Archer had also been recently released from jail. Surely with this additional information the Knoxville police would take Darby's concerns seriously.

"Do you think it's worth it to take these straight to the police?"

Darby had a point. Eyeing the clock, he noted it was just after eight. "We'd get the second shift, and your cable incident happened during the day." He shrugged. "I personally think it's better to wait until morning. That way we can talk directly to the guy in charge of the investigation."

"I can go with that," Darby agreed. "So back to the motel?"

"Yeah." It was still early, the sun bright, but he figured she was stiff and sore from her fall. They climbed into the car. "We can meet for breakfast in the morning, they offer it free to guests from six to eight."

The corner of Darby's mouth tipped up in a smile.

"What?" he asked.

She gave a rueful shake of her head. "Before I knew you, my foster sister Hailey and I used to sneak into motels to help ourselves to the free continental breakfasts." Her smile faded. "Yeah, it was wrong to steal, but we were young and couldn't get decent jobs because we didn't have IDs."

"I don't blame you, Darby. You did what was necessary in order to survive." He wasn't innocent in that respect either. But her mention of an ID brought up another question. "Is your last name still Walsh?"

"Yes. The staff at the halfway house helped me get the proper paperwork so I could get my ID and driver's license." There was a long pause before she added, "Although if you want the truth, I'm not really sure what my last name really is."

"You're not?"

"Nope." She pulled into the parking lot of the motel and parked near the lobby. "I was placed in foster care at an early age. I'm sure that I had a last name at some point, but I was only seven when I went to live with the Preacher and his wife. If they had paperwork on me, I'm sure it was lost the night of the fire."

"Fire?" This was the first he was hearing about the Preacher and the fire.

"Long story." She waved him off and slid out of the car. He followed, coming over to stand beside her. "And irrelevant. I vaguely remembered the name Walsh, but I can't swear it was mine or just something I heard along the way."

He could easily see how that might happen. "Well, Darby Walsh, it's nice to meet you."

She gave him an odd look.

"This is the first time we're meeting as law-abiding citizens of Knoxville, Tennessee." He held out his hand. "And I'm really glad to meet you."

She shook her head as if he'd lost his mind but reached for his hand. Their fingers entwined, sending a shaft of awareness stabbing through him. "Nice to meet you, too, Gage Killion."

He didn't let go of her hand for a long moment. When she gently pulled away, he let out a deep breath, reminding himself to stay cool.

A flash of movement caught the corner of his eye. He instinctively grabbed Darby, protectively pulling her down and curling his body around hers a nanosecond before the sound of gunfire echoed around them.

"Oomph," Darby said as they hit the ground.

"This way," he urged, pulling her toward the narrow space between the building and her car. He waited for another round of gunfire but heard nothing but the sound of their gasping breaths.

"Are you okay?" he whispered.

"Yes. You?"

He nodded and took a moment to drag in a ragged breath. "We need to call the police."

"How did Reyes find us?" Darby asked.

"It's my fault," he admitted hoarsely, his gaze landing on his white pickup truck, the crumpled bumper in plain sight. He should have gotten a rental car rather than using his own vehicle.

The shooter must have recognized his truck and had waited for him to return to the motel.

His lapse in judgment had almost gotten Darby killed.

CHAPTER FOUR

Gage had saved her life.

Darby crouched beside him, humbly grateful for his strong presence. If she'd had any doubts about Tyrone or Archer coming after them, they were gone now. No way was the gunfire aimed at them outside the motel an accident.

Scary to think of how close they'd been to being injured or killed. Those seconds were a blur, but it seemed as if Gage knew what was going to happen, the way he'd dragged her down just before the gunshot rang out.

"Gunfire at the Knotty Pine Motel." Gage was speaking into his phone. "We're not hurt, but we're pinned behind a car. We need the police here, ASAP."

She'd been so shaken by the gunfire it hadn't occurred to her to call 911. Darby was doubly glad she'd insisted that Edith take Leo away for the rest of the week. He was probably having a great time at the water park.

She and Gage needed to make sure Reyes and Archer never got near their son.

"I'm sorry, Darby." Gage's expression was steeped in guilt. "This is all my fault."

That was the second time he'd said that. "How is it possibly your fault? You don't own a gun, do you?"

"No. But don't you see? Reyes or Archer must have recognized my truck, along with the damaged rear bumper." He ruefully shook his head. "I should have used a rental car."

"That would have been expensive," she pointed out. "And your rear-end collision didn't happen on this side of town, right?"

"No, it happened on my way home from work, but that doesn't mean they couldn't track me down."

"How could they do that?" They were huddled so close together she could see the tiny flecks of gold around the irises of his green eyes. "I mean, even if they had your license plate number, tracking you here would have been difficult."

"I don't know." Gage looked sick to his stomach, and she found herself wanting to comfort him. No matter how they'd been found, she didn't blame Gage. Especially after the way he'd risked his life to save hers. "Maybe they followed me here."

"When did you get into town?" she asked.

"Last night." He rubbed the back of his neck. "My plan was to come talk to you this morning. It's why I was at the adventure park when your cable snapped."

"That's a pretty tight timeline," she pointed out. "There wouldn't have been enough time for Reyes or Archer to have discovered my routine. Especially since I rotate jobs at the adventure park. I do a week of zip-lining, then a week on the balance bridges, then a week on the hiking trails." The more she thought about it, the more she felt certain these guys had been in the area longer than a day or two. "This isn't your fault, Gage."

"Yeah, it is—" He stopped abruptly when the police cruiser came barreling toward them with lights and sirens.

She gave him a quick hug, then watched as two uniformed officers wearing vests emerged from the squad. Since there hadn't been any more gunfire since the initial shot, Darby felt certain the shooter was long gone.

But she and Gage didn't move from their hiding spot until the police officers approached. "Gage Killion?" one of them asked.

"Yes." Gage slowly stood, taking her hand to draw her up beside him. "And this is Darby Walsh."

So much for going to the police department in the morning to tell their story. Looked as if they'd be in for a long night of answering questions.

Clinging to Gage's hand, she was profoundly grateful she wouldn't be going through all of this alone. Not that she wanted Gage to be in danger, but having him at her side gave her the strength she'd need to get through this.

It was during times of stress that she struggled with. Not that she intended to break her sobriety, but it wasn't always as easy to ignore the temptation when your world was crumbling around you.

Darby vowed to remain strong for Leo's sake. And her own. After the officers took their names and statements, the cops fanned out to search the immediate area. She and Gage went into the motel lobby to wait and watch. It didn't take long for one of the officers to find the slug embedded in the side of the motel.

Proof that the gunshot had been meant for them and wasn't a story sprouted from their fertile imagination.

"I'm not sure we should stay here tonight," Gage

murmured in a low voice. "It's not worth the risk that Reyes and or Archer might come back to finish the job."

"Okay, but where can we go?" She hesitated, then suggested, "We could take a rideshare back to my townhouse. You can sleep in Leo's room."

He offered a wry smile. "As much as I'd love nothing better than to sleep in our son's room, I'm not sure heading back to your townhouse is any safer." His smile faded. "We'll definitely take a rideshare to minimize the possibility of being followed, but we need to find somewhere else to go."

She knew he was considering another budget motel. Which was fine, aside from the cost. "Okay," she agreed, trying not to wince at the dent this would put in her meager savings.

The officers returned, and the older guy took the lead. "We'd like you to come down to the station to discuss this further."

"That's fine," Gage agreed. "Although it would be nice to know what your investigation into the Great Outdoor Adventure Park cable incident revealed. Did you find proof that someone tampered with it?"

The cops exchanged a look. "I don't have that information."

"The cable breaking was the first attempt to hurt me, and this gunfire was the second," Darby said, doing her best not to sound accusatory. "If you guys can't figure out what's going on, I may not live through the third attempt."

"She's right," Gage agreed. "And I was run off the road two days ago too. I think it's pretty clear someone is coming after us."

"Which is why we'd like you to come to the precinct," the older cop said.

"Fine. Let's go." Darby couldn't deny being anxious to get out of there. "I'd like to grab my duffel bag."

"Actually, I have some personal things here that I'd like to take with us too." Gage glanced at the officers. "Can you give me five minutes?"

"Sure," the younger cop agreed. The older cop simply scowled.

Darby accompanied Gage to his room and waited for him to pack his bag. Within minutes, they were back inside the motel lobby with their things.

She and Gage were put in the back seat of the squad, with the metal grate separating them from the two officers. A flashback of the time she'd been arrested hit hard, and she pressed a hand to her stomach in an attempt to ward off the urge to throw up.

Six years suddenly seemed like yesterday. When Gage reached over to take her hand, she glanced at him in surprise.

"I know it's rough," he whispered. "But we're the victims here."

She nodded, understanding he felt the same way about being in the back of the police car. If it wasn't for the fact that they needed to escape the motel without being followed, Darby sensed Gage would have insisted on driving separately.

It was a humble reminder of how far she'd come since that fateful day. And how little it would take to send her stumbling back in time.

When they arrived at the East Knoxville police station, she and Gage were split up, each taken into a different interrogation room. Darby tightly clasped her hands in her lap, trying to fight a surge of panic.

Gage was right, they were the victims here. But, deep

down, she knew they could never completely erase their past mistakes.

Despite the way they'd both turned their lives around, staying clean, working jobs, staying far away from their former drug addict friends, their respective criminal records would be with them forever.

And there wasn't a single thing they could do to change that.

GAGE WORRIED about how Darby was holding up as he eyed the older of the two cops sitting across from him. The guy's last name was Crow, and weirdly, Gage considered him to be just like the opportunistic bird.

"You served four years for drug dealing," Crow said.

Gage refused to be baited. "Was that a question?"

Crow glared at him. "And you believe the guy you ratted out has come to seek revenge."

"Yes. Tyrone Reyes and or Niles Archer." He wanted to cooperate, but this was feeling less like a questioning session and more like an interrogation.

"And have you seen either of these two men?" Crow asked.

"No." Gage leaned forward. "But you found the slug in the side of the motel. And there's proof Darby's cable broke, nearly killing her. I don't have to see them to know one or both of them are out there."

"You're telling me these are the only two men on the planet who have a beef against you?" Crow's expression was skeptical. "You were a drug dealer. I'm sure there are plenty of others out there who might want to hurt you."

Gage suppressed a sigh. "But these are the two men

who were ratted out by both me and Darby. Sure, I might have more enemies out there, but not her."

"From what I can tell, she ratted you out," Crow said with a smirk. "I find it interesting you two are hanging out together."

"Darby's turning me in to the police was the best thing that could have happened to me." He looked Crow dead in the eye. "I'm a different person now than I was back then." Thanks to the Bible study he'd done with Pastor Davies.

The cop shrugged. "If you say so."

Gage battled a wave of frustration, holding on to his temper with an effort. Once he'd have given in to the urge to wipe the smirk off the cop's face, but he managed to refrain. Despite finding the bullet lodged in the wall at the motel, the guy wasn't taking this attempt against them seriously. All because of Gage's criminal background. "That's not important," he said tersely. "The fact that someone tried to shoot us is the issue here. And no matter what my criminal record says, I have a right to be treated with respect. So does Darby Walsh."

Crow's eyes narrowed, but then he shrugged. "Of course. Do you have anything else to add to your statement?"

"No." Gage considered pulling the two articles they'd printed in the library from his pocket but deemed it a waste of time. Maybe the day shift officer looking into the zip line cable would be more interested in the recent gunfire. Crow couldn't obviously care less.

"Then you're free to go." Crow stood, staring down at him for a long moment. "See that you stay on the straight and narrow while you're staying in my neck of the woods. You still have three months left of probation. You cross the line, I'll toss you right back in jail."

"Yes, sir." Gage refused to let the cop get to him. After four years in prison, he was used to being talked down to, being treated as scum of the earth. The crimes he'd committed meant he'd deserved jail time, no question about that. But he wasn't a criminal any longer. And he didn't buy into the old adage that once a criminal, always a criminal.

Gage followed Crow from the room, glancing around for Darby. Crow led him down the hall to the small lobby. "You can wait for your girlfriend here."

He didn't bother to correct the guy. Instead, he leaned against the wall to wait. He hoped the fact that Darby's interview was taking longer meant the officer was doing a thorough job of obtaining any and all critical information.

Fifteen minutes later, Darby joined him. "How long have you been waiting here?" she asked with a frown.

"Not long. How did it go? Did you get any insight into the zip line cable incident?"

"No, but Officer Rauland agreed to check into that for me." She sent him a sidelong glance as they walked outside. "How did your conversation go?"

"Not sure Officer Crow cares whether they arrest the shooter or not, but at least the attempt against us has been documented." He shrugged. "It's better than nothing."

Her gaze softened. "I'm sorry. It really sucks to be treated like a loser."

He offered a lopsided smile. "Like I said, at least the shooting is on record. And if the investigation stalls, we can always go up the chain of command." During his four-year stint in prison, he'd only filed one complaint. Looking back, he figured the only reason he'd gotten the warden's attention at all was because Pastor Davies had probably put in a good word for him.

Pushing the memories aside, he used his phone to call for a rideshare.

"Where are we going?" Darby asked, sticking close to his side.

"I saw a sign for a place called the Rustic Roadhouse." It was one of the few that appeared to be in his price range. "We should be fine there for the rest of the night."

"Okay." Darby glanced nervously over her shoulder. "If you think so."

He loosely draped his arm around her. "We're going to be okay, Darby."

She leaned against him, and he wasn't going to lie, he liked having Darby close. She'd been staying near his side since the gunfire, out of fear most likely. Especially since she'd made it clear she was not interested in picking up where they'd left off.

In a way, he was glad about that. Oh, he was still attracted to her, more than any other woman he'd met in the nearly two years he'd been out of jail. Yet he and Darby had both changed in the six years they were apart.

Changed for the better. And he secretly hoped this time together would provide the foundation for them having a fresh start.

For Leo's sake.

"Has Edith checked in with you?" He glanced at her. "I'd like to know she and Leo are doing okay."

"Yes. She texted that Leo loved the water park and fell asleep without issue." Her gaze softened. "I miss it when I don't get to tuck him in at night."

"I can imagine." He wanted to ask if there might be a time when he'd be allowed to tuck Leo into bed, but their rideshare car pulled up.

"Gage?" the driver called.

"Yes." He drew Darby toward the waiting car and opened the door for her. When they were both seated, he leaned forward. "Please take us to the Burger Barn located on Elm Street."

Darby frowned. "I thought," she began, but he squeezed her hand.

"It's close enough to the motel," he said in a low voice. "We can walk from there."

She nodded and clutched his hand tightly.

Maybe he was being paranoid, but after two attempts against Darby in one day, he wasn't willing to take any chances. Especially not with her life.

He wanted to ask about which water park Leo and Edith were staying at but decided to keep his questions about their son to a minimum.

For now.

The trip didn't take long, and Gage added a modest tip as they climbed from the car. "Thanks."

The driver nodded, looking disappointed at the short trip.

Gage continued to hold Darby's hand. "Let's cut through behind the fast-food joint," he suggested. "According to my map app, the motel is on the next block."

She nodded, and together they cut through the narrow space between two buildings. Gage doubted they were followed from the police station, but he didn't waste any time ducking into the lobby of the Rustic Roadhouse.

"Two rooms please." He smiled at the front desk clerk, a woman who was just a few years older than he was.

"I'm sorry, I only have one room available, but it has two double beds." The clerk eyed them curiously as if wondering why he'd requested separate rooms.

"Oh, okay. Thanks anyway." He turned from the desk, but Darby tugged on his arm.

"We can share the room," she said. "Platonically."

He was surprised by her offer. "Are you sure?"

She nodded. "Cheaper to split the cost, right?"

"Okay, we'll take it," he told the clerk. He handed over his debit card, determined to pay for the room himself.

"Oh, we only accept credit cards," the clerk said.

He nodded, having heard the same thing at the Knotty Pine. "I don't have a credit card, sorry. But the last place I went to made an exception."

"I don't know," the clerk didn't look convinced.

"I have a credit card," Darby said, pulling it from her purse. "Here."

It burned to accept Darby's help financially. "I would like to pay," he insisted. "You can have her card on file in case there's damage, but I would like to pay with my debit card."

"That's fine." The clerk took both Darby's credit card and his debit card. Five minutes later, they were provided two room keys. "You're in room 201 on the second floor."

"Thanks." He took one of the keys and walked outside with Darby. There was a rickety old elevator, but they chose to take the stairs to the second floor.

"It's not bad." Darby glanced around as he set her bag on the bed closest to the bathroom.

"We've stayed in far worse." The comment slipped out before he could stop it. He hadn't meant to remind her of their previous relationship.

"True." Darby didn't meet his gaze, and he wondered if she regretted agreeing to the arrangement. "Do you mind if I use the bathroom first?"

"Help yourself." When she disappeared into the bathroom, he dropped onto the edge of the bed and let out a heavy sigh.

Keeping an emotional distance from Darby was proving to be more difficult than he'd anticipated. More so now that they were sharing a motel room. The more time they spent together, the more he liked and admired how she'd turned herself around.

His only regret was not knowing about his son. What if he'd never come to see Darby? He still wouldn't have known about Leo.

God had sent him here to find his son. And to keep Darby and Leo safe. Thinking back to the hint of movement he'd glimpsed, how he'd known they were in danger, only cemented his belief that God was guiding him.

"Your turn." Darby dropped her bag onto the floor next to her bed. She wore a T-shirt and shorts as pajamas. They were nothing special, but he couldn't help thinking she looked incredible.

"Thanks." He took his bag into the bathroom, too, to change in private. By the time Gage emerged, he found Darby curled up in bed with her eyes closed. He doubted she'd fallen asleep so quickly but respected her wishes by easing toward his own bed and shutting off the lights.

But sleep eluded him. He brought Leo's image into his mind and tried to imagine what it might be like to hug the little guy. He thought about Darby and how difficult it must have been for her to raise him without any financial support from him. He was glad she had Edith, the way he'd been given Pastor Davies.

"No!" Darby's abrupt cry had him bolting out of bed.

"What is it?" He looked around wildly. "Are you okay?"

Darby blinked and looked around in confusion. "Where are we?"

"The Rustic Roadhouse." His heart was still hammering in his chest. "Relax, Darby, you must have had a bad dream."

"Yes. A nightmare." She didn't relax, though, but sat up and pushed her hair from her face. "I dreamed Reyes found Leo."

"I'm sorry." He sat beside her. "Leo is safe with Edith."

"I know." She let out a heavy sigh. "It just—seemed so real."

He wanted to comfort her, but he didn't want to give her the wrong impression of his intentions. She took the decision from him by leaning toward him, resting her head on his shoulder. He wrapped his arm around her and hugged her close.

"I'm sorry this is happening," he whispered. "I hope and pray the police find Reyes and Archer before they can do any more damage."

"Me too." She didn't say anything more for a long moment. "Gage? Thanks for saving my life."

"Anytime."

"No, really." She lifted her head to peer at him through the darkness, broken only by the ambient light from outside. "I never expected you to shield me with your body like that. I'm glad the shooter missed."

"I'll always protect you, Darby."

"I believe you." She looked at him for a minute, then leaned forward to kiss him. It was likely a gesture of gratitude, but the moment their lips touched, the kiss morphed into something more. Something dangerous.

The hot flare of gut-clenching desire.

CHAPTER FIVE

Darby hadn't anticipated the spontaneous combustion that resulted from her kissing Gage. It seemed impossible to still want him as much—no, *more* than before. For several seconds she simply clung to him, reveling in their embrace, but all too soon, Gage lifted his head, breaking off from their kiss.

"I—uh, we can't—" He was comically at a loss for words.

"I know." She understood what he meant. They were sharing the motel room, platonically. As per her insistence. This—whatever it was—couldn't happen. "I'm sorry. I stepped over the line."

"No, you were only trying to thank me." Gage raked his hand through his hair and staggered upright. "I turned your simple kiss into something more."

He was wrong, their kiss had changed into something deeper because the two of them together were like a match to a flame. But now that she was thinking more clearly, she appreciated his restraint. Gage's intent to protect her was sweet, but she wasn't interested in picking up where they'd left off.

Gage was a complication she didn't need. Especially if he wanted to be an ongoing part of Leo's life. What if things didn't work out between them? They were forever linked by their adorable son.

No, she couldn't take the risk.

"Are you okay now?" Gage's question confused her for a moment before she realized he was referring to her nightmare.

"Yes, thanks." She turned away and crawled back into bed, snuggling beneath the covers, listening as Gage did the same. The memory of their kiss was too fresh in her mind, and she knew sleep wouldn't come easily.

If at all.

After an hour of staring at the wall, she finally fell back to sleep. No nightmares this time, thankfully. But when she woke up, her first thought was of her son.

She'd never spent this much time away from Leo. When she took the occasional three-day weekend off work, she and Leo would do things together in order to provide Edith a well-deserved break.

It had barely been twenty-four hours, and she already missed the little boy's hugs.

Okay, enough with the pity party. Leo's safety was the only thing that mattered.

She sat up in bed, noticing Gage's bed was empty. For a moment, she wondered if he'd decided to leave, but then she dismissed the notion. This new and improved version of Gage wouldn't do that. Not after throwing himself in front of her to protect her from gunfire.

Sitting up, Darby decided to take advantage of the ability to use the bathroom. Scooping up her duffel from the floor, she winced as her entire body was sore from her fall. Ignoring the discomfort, she quickly brushed her teeth, showered, and dried her hair. When she realized she was taking more time with her hair than usual, she tossed the brush back into her bag with a sigh of disgust.

This wasn't about looking nice for Gage. She needed to stay focused on doing whatever they could to find Reyes or Archer.

The motel door opened, and Gage came in carrying a bag of food. "Hi, how did you sleep?"

"Great." Not really, but she wasn't about to admit that memories of their kiss had kept her up. "You went to get breakfast?"

"Yeah, they don't offer a free one here. I hope I didn't wake you." He set the bag of food down, then reached in to draw out two cups of coffee.

She took the coffee from him, their fingers brushing ever so slightly. "How much do I owe you?"

He hesitated. "I know you wanted to pay for half the expenses, but breakfast is on me."

"Gage . . ." She sighed. "Are you going to keep doing this for the rest of the day?"

"Probably." He shrugged and smiled. "I can't help it. I keep thinking of the way you raised Leo for these past five years all on your own. Paying for a few meals and our motel room is the least I can do."

"That was my choice," she pointed out, taking a sip of her coffee.

"It wasn't exactly a choice, considering I was in jail." He waved a hand. "It doesn't matter, Darby. That's all in the past. Let's just move forward from here, deal?"

"Deal." There was no point in arguing. She crossed over to peer inside the bag. "Looks like you remembered my favorite breakfast sandwich too."

His expression turned serious. "I remember everything, Darby. Even the things I did that I'd rather forget."

She grimaced. "I know, I feel the same way sometimes. Thankfully, having Leo keeps me distracted from dwelling on the past."

"I'm glad you and Leo are doing so well." Gage pulled out their sandwiches and set them on the small table. She joined him, surprised when he bowed his head and closed his eyes.

Was he—praying?

A memory of the Preacher ranting and raving as they knelt before him flashed in her mind. She shoved it aside and waited for Gage to finish before taking a bite of her sandwich.

"I did Bible study in prison with Pastor Davies."

She looked at him in surprise. "And what—it changed your life?"

"Yes." He met her gaze head-on. "I know you mentioned not believing in God, and I can understand where you're coming from. But I know God is watching over us, Darby. He was there last night; I sensed something bad was going to happen just before the gunshot rang out."

It was tempting to refute his claim, but she had noticed Gage's quick reaction. She didn't believe in God, but she didn't believe Gage was psychic either. "You probably have honed instincts from being in prison."

"Maybe." Gage took a bite of his sandwich, chewing thoughtfully. "I know you suffered abuse when you were young, the same as I did. But you never mentioned that abuse involved a Preacher."

"Yeah, well, the Preacher claimed to be doing God's will, which included making us sleep on the floor of the cellar and kneeling for hours on end as he screamed and hit us with a switch. So yeah, I'm pretty sure I'm not interested in hearing about your God."

"I'm sorry you had to endure that." Gage's expression was full of empathy. "But you should know God isn't about anger and abuse. He's loving, kind, and forgiving."

"Whatever." Time to change the subject. "What's our plan for the day? Still heading over to the police station?"

"I think so, although I'm not sure we'll get very far." He sipped his coffee. "I was thinking we could take the photo of Reyes and Archer and show them to your co-workers at the adventure park. See if anyone noticed either of them hanging around."

It wasn't a bad idea. "All right." She finished her sandwich. "But it will be a hike to get there, unless you're planning on using another rideshare."

He hesitated. "I guess I'd rather walk, if that's okay with you."

"I don't mind. I'm used to physical activity." Granted, her muscles were achy from her fall, but she wasn't going to let that stop her.

"Even after your collision with the tree?"

"Yeah, I'm okay."

He gestured toward his duffel bag. "I have over-the-counter stuff, like ibuprofen."

"No thanks." Logically, she knew ibuprofen wasn't addictive, but she'd made a point of not taking any medications for any reason. Deep down, she was afraid that once she went down that path, she'd break down and stray into dangerous territory.

"Okay, the bigger question is whether we stay here another night." Gage eyed her over the rim of his coffee cup. "I don't think it's safe for you to return to your townhouse."

"I know." She swept a gaze around the motel room. "We can stay here one more night."

Gage nodded. "We'll stop in the lobby on our way to the adventure park."

"Speaking of which, I'm supposed to go back to work tomorrow." A shiver of apprehension skipped down her spine. "This is the height of the tourist season, I can't leave them shorthanded."

"I thought the zip lines were down anyway?" Gage asked. "If so, it would seem logical they wouldn't miss one more staff person."

"I'll check with my boss." It was the most she could agree to. "I can't lose my job, Gage. I need to pay my portion of the rent."

"I understand." He leaned forward, bracing his elbows on the table. "But you should also know that I'm going to help pay for Leo's expenses. As soon as this mess is behind us, I'll make arrangements to have a portion of my paycheck deposited in your bank account."

She wanted to protest, but now that Gage knew about Leo, there wasn't a way to go back to the way things were. "We'll figure that out later."

"Yeah, we will." His tone was firm. He gathered their empty wrappers, tossing them into the garbage. "Ready?"

"Yes." She wasn't, really, but sitting here wasn't an option. "What if no one recognizes Reyes or Archer?"

"We broaden our search," Gage responded. "Someone somewhere has seen one of these two men. We just need to figure out where they are."

"Is that all?" She'd meant to be teasing, but the words sounded flat and hard. "Sorry," she quickly added. "Guess I'm grumpy this morning."

"I know." Gage opened the motel room door, gesturing for her to head out first.

As they walked back to the police station, Darby couldn't help feeling depressed at the insurmountable task before them.

They had no leads, no proof that Reyes or Archer were responsible for the incidents that had nearly killed them.

And she couldn't help worrying that the former convicts would succeed in their next attempt before anyone was the wiser.

GAGE SHARED DARBY'S FRUSTRATION, but he didn't know what to say to make her feel better. Sure, maybe they'd find someone at the adventure park that remembered seeing Reyes or Archer, but would that be enough for the police to put out a BOLO for the two men?

Somehow, he doubted it.

After a quick stop in the motel lobby to pay for another day, Gage led the way outside. The Tennessee sun was warm and had already broken through the early morning mist. The Smoky Mountains loomed tall and majestic behind them. He rather liked this area of the city, located closer to the woods and mountains, despite the obvious catering to tourism. The construction company he worked for, Morehead Construction, was headquartered in the western part of the city, where more of the residential housing was located.

When his week of vacation was up, he'd have to go back. Knoxville wasn't as large as Nashville, but even being on the other side of the city from where Darby and Leo lived would seem as if he were on another planet. Working long hours would make it difficult to drive back and forth to see them on a daily basis. And he normally worked Saturdays, too, if overtime was offered.

But he remained determined to be involved in his son's life. Maybe he'd find a small apartment here, close to them. At least that way he could see Leo more often.

Darby too.

Ah, Darby. He'd had a hard time sleeping after their explosive kiss. Finding the strength to end their embrace had been difficult. But he refused to repeat the mistakes of the past.

They'd jumped all too quickly into an intimate relationship. One he couldn't regret since Leo was the outcome. This time, though, he wanted to do better. To be the man Darby deserved.

To make a commitment.

Although Darby didn't feel the same way. He told himself they had plenty of time, but deep down, he couldn't ignore the sense of urgency. He'd missed five years of Leo's life; he didn't want to miss a day more.

They needed to find Reyes and Archer as soon as humanly possible.

"Are you planning to share the articles we printed on Reyes and Archer with the police?" Darby asked.

He glanced at her. "If they seem to be taking these attempts seriously, yes. Last night, I didn't bother with Officer Crow."

"Maybe we should head to the adventure park first, then." Darby spread her hands. "If we find someone who recognizes them, we'll have something new to tell the police, rather than simply rehashing what is already on record."

"Good idea," he said, shooting her an admiring glance. "I should have thought of that."

"Well, it's the only thing we can do to find these guys, right?"

"Yeah." He had another plan in mind, but Darby wouldn't like it since it involved her going to stay with Leo and Edith while he used himself as bait to draw Reyes and Archer out of hiding.

As a law-abiding citizen, he wanted to give the police the opportunity to do their job and get these guys. But he wasn't naïve enough to think the cops would fall over themselves to help a former convict. A guy who was still on parole for the next three months.

They switched course to head back to the adventure park. "Tell me about your boss."

"Kent Jacobs?" Darby looked at him in surprise. "What about him?"

"Is he a decent guy to work for?"

She shrugged. "Yeah, mostly. He's okay. I've had worse bosses."

"Will he give us a hard time about showing the photos to your co-workers?" They could do it on the sly, but he preferred being up-front and honest.

"Hmm. Good question." Darby sighed. "Probably not. I mean, he would if the police were the ones showing the pictures, but he'll likely lecture me about not staying home to rest after the fall."

"Okay, then we'll need to approach your co-workers without his knowing." Gage glanced at the large sign proclaiming the Great Adventure Outdoor Park. "Maybe we start with the guy you were working with on the zip line."

"Teddy O'Neil?" She looked doubtful. "I doubt he saw Reyes or Archer. If so, he'd have reported that to the police."

"Not if he happened to see one of them in passing,"

Gage insisted.

"Okay, but I'm not sure where he's stationed, we were both slated to work the zip lines all week."

"We'll talk to whoever we can, then." Gage knew this wasn't the time to be picky. For all they knew, Teddy had been given the day off too.

"I think we should start at the balance bridges," Darby said. "They're located a fair distance from the main building; we'll be less likely to run into Kent."

"Works for me."

They approached the park, and Gage suddenly realized they wouldn't be allowed inside without paying, until Darby jutted to the right, taking a shortcut to avoid the main entrance.

The woods were alive with squawking birds and buzzing insects. Gage followed as Darby cut a path through the brush toward the balance bridges. He could see them up ahead and was relieved to recognize Teddy was among the workers dressed in harnesses and helmets for protection.

"Teddy?" Darby's voice was soft. The kid looked around in confusion until she lifted a hand. "Over here."

"Darby?" Teddy jumped down from the low platform. Gage noticed it wasn't nearly as high as the zip lining one had been. "What are you doing here?" The kid eyed him warily. "You're the one who asked for Darby's address."

"Yes, and I appreciate you giving it to me."

"Teddy, this is a friend of mine, Gage Killion. Gage, Teddy O'Neil." She made quick introductions. "I have a quick question for you, Teddy, then I'll let you get back to work. Have you seen either of these two men?" She offered the printed photos to Teddy.

"We'd like to know if they visited the park recently," Gage added.

Teddy took a moment to peer at the grainy photos. "This guy looks familiar," the kid said, pointing to Reyes's mug shot. "I can't say for sure where I saw him, he could have been a guest here."

"Really?" Darby looked excited. "Do you remember when you may have seen him?"

Teddy grimaced and shook his head. "Sometime late last week, maybe. I don't know. Why are you asking? Do you think he's responsible for tampering with the zip line cable?"

"We don't know, we're just trying to figure out if either of these guys have been in the area," Gage interjected before Darby could respond. "Don't jump to conclusions."

"You're showing me a mug shot of some criminal, it's no stretch to think he's involved with what happened to Darby." Teddy scowled at him, and it took Gage a moment to realize the kid had a crush on Darby.

"Hey, it's okay, Teddy." Darby rested her hand on Teddy's arm. "Gage is trying to help me. Who's working the balance bridge with you?"

"Steve Auckland," Teddy answered without taking his gaze from Gage.

"Do you think we could talk to him? See if he recognizes these guys?" Darby asked. "I'd really appreciate your help on this, Teddy."

The kid finally turned toward her. "Yeah, sure thing. I'll get him for you."

"Thanks, Teddy." Darby dropped her hand, and the kid climbed back up onto the platform. A few minutes later, another guy came over, roughly the same age as Teddy.

Darby went through the same spiel with Steve Auckland. The only difference was that this guy didn't seem to have a crush on her.

"This guy looks familiar." He tapped the photo of Reyes. "I think he was here last Friday."

"Doing what?" Gage asked.

The kid looked at him. "He was in my early morning hiking group. We traversed the Willow Point Trail."

Gage eyed the kid with interest. "You're certain about that?"

Steve shrugged. "I tend to remember faces, and the thing that struck me the most was that this guy didn't seem like much of a hiker. It wasn't that he was out of shape or anything, but he had a lot of skin art and wore sneakers rather than hiking boots."

This was the first concrete lead they'd gotten on Reyes, and Gage tried to temper his excitement. "The other guy wasn't with him?"

"Nah. Don't remember seeing him at all." Steve glanced at Darby. "Thought you were off because you got hurt?"

"I'm trying to walk off the aches and pains," Darby said with a smile. "Thanks for the information."

"Sure." Steve turned away.

When they were alone, Gage whispered to Darby, "Where's the Willow Point Trail? Is it close enough to hike it?"

"Yeah, but we don't have any hiking gear," she pointed out. "It's crazy to hike without water at the very least."

"We don't have to go far, I just want to see the area." Gage reached for her hand. "After that, we'll head back to the police station."

"All right." She gestured to the left. "This way."

Gage followed Darby as she once again cut through the woods. Behind them, he could hear the kids welcoming guests to the balance bridge. When he turned to glance over his shoulder, the trees obscured his view.

Darby was right about hiking without proper equipment, which made him think about why Reyes had signed up for the hike in the first place. To scope the place out? They were heading in a different direction from where the zip lines were located.

And how had Reyes known Darby would be working the zip lines on Monday? Or hadn't he cared who died that day?

"This is part of the Willow Point Trail," Darby said as they came across a path. "It starts close to the park lobby and heads up a good two miles."

"Can you imagine Reyes hiking two miles in sneakers?" He shook his head. "Seems out of character."

"I doubt Steve has a reason to lie." Darby frowned and headed up the trail. "How far do you want to go?"

Since he had absolutely no clue what to even look for, he shook his head. "Not far. I guess this was a stupid idea."

"Not stupid—" She stopped abruptly.

"What's wrong?" He stepped up beside her, trying to figure out what caught her attention.

"Who would do such a gruesome thing?" Darby's voice sounded faint. A terrible scent wafted toward him, and he finally noticed what had caught her attention.

A squirrel was impaled to a tree with two sharp sticks, hanging at eye level.

He grabbed Darby's hand and drew her away from the horrific sight, taking several steps off the trail to hide in the brush. "Stay down," he whispered.

She didn't answer, her hand pressed to her stomach as if holding the contents back with an effort.

Gage swept a gaze over the area, feeling certain Reyes had done this. And could still be out there, somewhere.

CHAPTER SIX

Don't throw up. Don't throw up.

Darby did her best to block the ghastly image from her mind. While living in the woods after escaping the Preacher's cabin, she was no stranger to seeing dead animals. The circle of life meant she and Hailey had stumbled across many dead squirrels, chipmunks, and rabbits taken down by a larger predator. They'd even eaten a few rabbits themselves in order to stay alive as they'd made their way from North Carolina through the Smoky Mountains and into Tennessee.

But there was nothing natural about the squirrel being impaled on the tree. It had been done on purpose.

By human hands.

"Are you okay?" Gage's mouth was next to her ear, his voice low so it wouldn't carry. He had his arm around her shoulders, holding her protectively. Once again, she was thankful he was there with her. In the short time they'd been reunited, she'd found herself leaning on his strength more than ever.

She swallowed and gave a jerky nod. "Reyes?"

"Maybe, but it's weird, don't you think?" He was still speaking in a low voice. "He wouldn't know we'd take this trail to find it."

He made a good point. Lots of visitors walked this trail, although there were other hiking trails too. It was very strange to consider Reyes had left his mark. And certainly he hadn't done this on Friday. The carcass was too fresh. In a matter of hours, the hawks and crows would take care of whatever was left. She shivered. "Maybe someone else killed it and left it there as a prank."

Gage didn't say anything for a long moment. "I don't like coincidences. Steve told us a man fitting Reyes's description took this hike on Friday. Today is Tuesday, and we find a squirrel embedded to a tree. It feels like a warning of some kind. Reyes must have been the one to do this, maybe hoping that if another hiker stumbled across it, they'd tell your boss and you'd hear about it, maybe check it out for yourself."

That was a lot of supposition, but she couldn't come up with anything better. Especially since the squirrel was killed after she'd crashed into a tree when the zip line broke. "Do you think Reyes is still out here?"

"It's hard to say." Gage glanced around the area. "You know this area better than I do. Is there another way out of here? Maybe a shortcut to a different trail?"

Having something constructive to consider helped steady her nerves. She nodded slowly. "The Hawk Eye Trail isn't far. It will be rough going through the woods, though. We'll make more noise than if we simply take the Willow Point Trail back down."

Gage took a long moment to consider their options. "We weren't hiking long, maybe fifteen minutes, so heading back down the trail seems reasonable." He rose to his feet. "Stay in front of me, Darby. I'll cover your back."

The thought of Reyes shooting Gage in the back brought on another wave of nausea. "Maybe we just stay here and call the police."

"About a dead squirrel?" Gage shook his head. "They can't do anything about that. For all we know kids could have been playing out here."

The idea of kids impaling the squirrel onto the tree wasn't much better than imagining Reyes doing the deed. But she understood what he meant. "Okay, let's go, then."

She stood and eased silently through the brush toward the trail. Gage followed close behind. Darby resisted the urge to look over her shoulder, concentrating instead on getting down the trail to civilization.

Being in a crowd of people was something she normally avoided if at all possible, but not now. She didn't want to put anyone else in danger, but she also didn't want to be alone. To this point, the attacks were targeted specifically at her and Gage.

If Reyes shot up an entire group of people, the police wouldn't rest until they tracked him down.

The urge to get to the police department had her increasing her pace, her body tense as she prepared for the worst. Gage didn't have any trouble keeping up, and she was reminded again at how much better he looked than the last time she'd seen him, six years ago.

Twenty-four hours before she'd been arrested.

Working construction had honed his muscles and tanned his skin. Streaks of gold shimmered in his brown hair, highlighted from his time in the sun. There was a lot to admire about Gage, and it occurred to her how unusual it was for two former druggies to have put their criminal pasts behind them.

Darby burst into the clearing near the adventure park office building. For the first time since seeing the squirrel, she relaxed, tension easing from her.

"We made it." She glanced at Gage as he stood beside her.

"Yeah." Gage still looked a bit antsy, sweeping his gaze over the area. "Let's go. We'll take a rideshare to the police station."

"Sounds good." She led the way down the adventure park to the main road. Within minutes, a car pulled up beside them.

"Gage?" the driver asked.

"Yes." Gage took one last look over his shoulder before following her into the car. She wondered if he'd heard someone moving along the trail behind them.

Gage gave the driver the address for the police station. The air-conditioning streaming from the vents felt nice against her sticky, sweaty skin.

She felt Gage's muscles relax as the driver pulled away. "Did you hear something back there?"

"No, but we were vulnerable to an attack." He reached over to take her hand. "I don't like knowing you're in danger, Darby."

"Back at you." She tried to smile. "But we're okay. And the police will surely follow up on Reyes."

"I hope so." Gage stared down at their joined hands for a long moment. "After we talk to the police, I think you should stay with Leo and Edith for the rest of the week."

For a fraction of a second, she wanted to agree. But she shook her head. "No, Gage. What if my going there puts them in danger?"

"I need to know you're safe, Darby." Gage's hand tightened on hers. "I don't like the way Reyes scoped out the adventure park last Friday, mere days before your cable broke."

Followed hours later by the gunfire outside the Knotty Pine Motel. She tightened her grip on his hand. "I don't like it either, but once the police find Reyes, the danger will be over."

"Yeah." Gage didn't sound convinced. "If they can tie him with evidence to the crimes."

That punctured the balloon of hope in her heart. For a moment, she considered asking Gage to go with her to stay with Leo and Edith, but then she realized that would only prolong the inevitable.

Even if they did disappear for a while, Reyes wasn't going to simply pick up his toys and go home. No, he'd hang out, watching and waiting for them to return.

Unless they left Knoxville to relocate somewhere else? She instinctively recoiled from that idea.

She liked her job and the townhouse she shared with Leo and Edith. Gage had a good job too. Leo had his preschool friends and would start kindergarten in the fall.

Not to mention her narcotics anonymous support group was here. It wouldn't be hard to find another program, they were located in almost every city, but she liked the group of people she met with each week.

The fact that she was already imagining a future with Gage, not a personal relationship but as Leo's father, surprised her. And made her more determined than ever to find a way to get Reyes behind bars.

Their rideshare driver let them off in front of the police station. Gage held her hand as they went inside, and she wondered if he needed the physical connection between them the same way she did.

"We'd like to talk to whoever is investigating the broken cable at the Great Outdoor Adventure Park," Gage announced. "Ms. Walsh is the victim in that near fatal event."

"Just a moment please." The woman behind the bullet-proof glass picked up a phone and spoke so softly Darby couldn't hear what she said. "Please wait, Detective Pride will be with you shortly."

"Thanks." Gage glanced at her. "Did you talk to a detective yesterday?"

"No. Just an officer. It's probably a good sign they've assigned a detective to the case."

Gage nodded. "Yeah. Although I would have thought he'd want to talk to you. Could be he tried to find you at the townhouse."

"Why not call me?" She patted her phone. "I still have my cell."

Gage frowned, but before he could say anything, a man roughly their age emerged from the locked door. "Ms. Walsh? I'm Detective Joel Pride."

"Darby, and this is a friend of mine, Gage Killion." She eyed the detective. "We'd both like to discuss the cable incident, among others."

He narrowed his gaze. "I believe the cable was nothing more than an accident, but we can certainly discuss it if you'd like." His tone belied his words. Pride didn't seem to want to talk with them at all, especially given the way he kept glancing at his watch.

"Yes, I would like to discuss it further," Darby said forcefully. "Hasn't anyone mentioned the gunfire at the Knotty Pine Motel?"

Pride sighed and stepped back. "This way." He raised his voice to reach the woman behind the desk. "We'll be in interview C."

"Okay," the woman agreed.

Darby continued clutching Gage's hand as they followed the detective through the door and down a narrow hallway. The fact that he'd so easily dismissed the cable as an accident bothered her. Especially after they'd almost been hit by gunfire.

As she dropped into a seat across from the detective, she found herself wondering what on earth she and Gage could do if the police didn't believe them.

GAGE INWARDLY SEETHED at Pride's dismissive tone but held his anger in check. He decided to let Darby take the lead, ready to jump in to help as needed.

"I've been working at the Great Outdoor Adventure Park for three years," Darby began. "Never once has a cable failed until yesterday morning."

"Zip lines are notoriously dangerous," Pride pointed out.

She lifted a hand. "You didn't let me finish. I have seen a cable wear down, begin to sag in the middle. That wasn't at all what happened here. The cables are also on a routine maintenance schedule, which was done just three months ago in the spring. We always gear up for the tourist season."

Gage almost smiled in satisfaction when the detective sat back in his seat with a thoughtful expression on his face.

"Furthermore, it wasn't long after that cable broke that Mr. Killion and I were outside the Knotty Pine Motel. You really think that someone shot at us by accident?" Darby waved an impatient hand. "Come on, it's clear someone is trying to hurt me. And Mr. Killion." She turned toward him. "Tell him about your rear-end collision."

He picked up the story. "Last weekend I was coming home from working a Saturday shift with the Morehead Construction company when a black SUV rear-ended me. I managed to stay on the road, and the driver took off. There's a police report on file about it, and my white truck still has a sizable dent in the rear bumper. Oh, and my truck is still parked at the Knotty Pine Motel, along with Ms. Walsh's sedan. I believe the same man, Tyrone Reyes, is responsible for all three incidents." He drew out the articles he and Darby had printed at the library, pushing them across the table.

"See this guy?" Darby tapped the picture of Reyes. "One of my co-workers believes he attended a nature hike on Friday. Three days before the zip line cable failed."

For the first time since they'd started their tale, Detective Pride looked interested. He leaned forward and looked at the mug shots of Reyes and Archer. "Why would this man try to hurt you?"

Gage drew in a breath, knowing this was where things would get sticky. "Because when I was arrested six years ago, I gave the state evidence of his drug running. He went to jail as a result of my testimony."

"And I mentioned his name to the police as well," Darby added. "Look, I know how this looks, both Gage and I have troubled pasts. But you need to know we've both put that behind us. We're working and staying clean. We learned Reyes is out of jail, maybe because he'd ratted someone out too. It's no stretch of the imagination to think he's come after us to settle a score."

A flash of annoyance crossed the detective's face. Gage knew it was because of his criminal record.

"Hey, attempted murder is still a big deal. Just because we were mixed up in something we shouldn't have been six years ago doesn't mean it's okay for someone to try to kill us now." He pinned the detective with a narrow look. "Maybe you don't realize that Ms. Walsh has a five-year-old son. Does that child deserve to lose his mother to this maniac?" He gestured to the article on Reyes. "And what if the kid gets in the way, huh? Are you going to sit back while some innocent kid dies because you didn't take us seriously?"

"I never said I wasn't taking your concerns seriously." Detective Pride backed down beneath his verbal assault. "I can see how these three incidents might be related."

Might? Gage had to bite his tongue.

"I'm curious as to whether or not Reyes is still on probation," Darby said. "It's possible he's with Archer, which would violate his probation, correct?"

"There's no evidence they're together," Pride countered. "What was the name of that employee who recognized Reyes? I'll talk to him."

"Steve Auckland. He's working the balance bridge today with Teddy O'Neil." Darby reached for the articles. "I would think you'd at least want to bring Reyes in for questioning. See if he has an alibi for the timeframe of the incidents."

"This isn't a TV show." There was a hint of derision in the detective's tone that set Gage's teeth on edge. "If I can verify that Reyes was at the park, I'll put out a BOLO for him." He stared at them. "Anything else?"

Darby glanced at him, silently asking if they should mention the impaled squirrel. Gage shook his head. "No, that's all." He rose, drawing Darby up beside him. "Thanks for your time."

"Yes, we do. I just hope you find Reyes before he tries to hurt us again," Darby added. "I would appreciate any updates in the case as well."

"Of course." Detective Pride joined them at the door. "I believe we have your number on file, Ms. Walsh."

"I would feel more comfortable if you'd take down Mr. Killion's number as well." Darby spoke politely, but her narrowed gaze indicated she wasn't happy. "He is as much a victim in this as I am. And we should both be included in any updates you're able to provide."

"Sure." Pride made a show of pulling out his notebook. "What's your number?"

Gage rattled it off, not believing for a moment the guy intended to keep them updated on his progress. Despite the fact that Pride did give them both copies of his business card.

Unfortunately, there wasn't anything else they could do now other than wait for the detective to validate with Steve Auckland that Reyes had been at the park on Friday. Gage hoped Steve took the detective up the trail far enough to see the impaled squirrel.

If it was still there. It could be ravaged by wildlife by now, or even removed by whoever had stuck it there.

The entire time he'd followed Darby down the trail there had been a nagging itch along the back of his neck.

As if someone was watching from deep in the woods.

Not that sitting and watching was Reyes's style. If the former drug dealer had been back there, Gage felt certain he'd have taken a shot at them. Especially since there wouldn't have been any witnesses.

In fact, he'd been braced for that to happen with each step they'd taken.

But now that they were safe, he figured the feeling had been nothing but sheer paranoia. Ironic that he needed to watch his back, and Darby's, more now than he had while in prison. Despite the horror stories some people told, he couldn't complain too much about how he'd lived over those four years. Thankfully, he'd been in a minimal security prison, away from those who committed crimes like murder and human trafficking.

If they could prove Reyes was involved in the attempts against them, Gage hoped the guy would do time in a maximum security facility.

Where he belonged.

He and Darby left the police station on foot. He was going through his savings at a fast rate and didn't want to call for yet another rideshare. "Are you hungry? We can find someplace to eat."

"That works." Darby glanced at him. "Do you think the detective will find Reyes?"

"I hope so."

"Yeah, but I don't have a lot of faith in him." Darby sighed and tucked a strand of hair behind her ear. "The minute he heard you did time his whole attitude changed."

"It's not the first time that's happened," he felt compelled to point out. "And probably won't be the last."

"It's not fair, Gage. The fact that you've turned your life around should count for something."

"No one said life was fair." He caught her hand. "You and I both know that all too well."

"Yeah." She grimaced. "Tell me about it."

He carefully broached the subject of faith, or her lack thereof. "I know it's hard to understand why God allows children like us to be abused. It's one of the aspects of faith I spoke to Pastor Davies about at length. You can see people living wonderful lives, seemingly unfazed. And yes, it truly isn't fair for some children to go hungry, be abused, die of cancer before their tenth birthday . . ."

There was a long pause before she looked at him. "And what did that pastor of yours have to say about that?"

"He agreed there is evil in the world and many suffer for it. Even Jesus was horribly abused and tortured before he was killed. And the reason God sent Jesus to live among us was to prove that if we loved and believed in God, we would be saved."

She didn't respond, and he hoped that meant she was considering what he'd said. They turned up a side street where a family-style restaurant was located.

"I still find it hard to believe that God would allow bad things to happen to children," she finally said. "They are the true innocents in all of this."

"I know, Darby." He offered a tired smile. "I agree it's difficult to comprehend but look at where we are now. Reyes and Archer aside, we've both risen above our respective pasts. We've moved on with our lives. You're raising a wonderful little boy. Think back to when we first met, did you ever think we'd be standing here like this?"

"No," she frankly admitted. "Never."

"Exactly. I believe God had a hand in our success. That maybe this was all a part of God's plan all along. That if we hadn't done those bad things, we may not be here today."

"Maybe." Her voice lacked conviction.

"Darby." He put a hand on her arm, stopping her progress. Having this discussion in the middle of the sidewalk wasn't optimal, but he needed to help her understand.

"If you and I hadn't met when we did, you wouldn't have Leo."

She gazed into his eyes for a moment, before looking away. "Believe me, Gage, I've often thought of that. Without Leo . . ." She shrugged. "I doubt I'd be alive. I was close to spiraling out of control back then. And I had no interest in changing until I discovered I was pregnant, shortly before my arrest." She put a hand over her lower abdomen as if remembering that moment. "I changed my life for Leo. And so far it's been working out. One day at a time, or so my counselor says."

"One day at a time," he agreed. "I was more about making money back then, but I did my share of drugs in an effort to forget."

She offered a crooked smile. "Me too. I'm glad we're beyond that now, Gage. At least for me, I have no intention of going back to those days."

"Me either." He released her arm so they could continue walking. "Darby, I know we have to wait until Reyes has been picked up by the cops, but I'd still like to get to know my son."

She nodded. "I've been thinking about that too. About how Leo deserves to know you are his father. Just"—she glanced at him—"don't hurt him, Gage."

Gage reared back as if she'd slapped him. "I would never lay a hand on him, Darby."

"No, that's not what I meant," she hastened to reassure. "I meant emotionally. Leo will need your ongoing support, not just on holidays or other special occasions, but the way all boys need their dads. Some day you may meet someone you want to have a family with, which is fine, but don't forget about him."

"I'll never forget about him." He was tempted to add

that right now the only person he was remotely interested in being with was her. The memory of their kiss still had the ability to steal his breath away.

Yet despite their heated kiss, Darby probably didn't feel the same way. In fact, he'd never come right out and asked if she was seeing anyone.

He was just about to ask her when he noticed a large SUV coming around the corner, faster than the side street speed limit allowed. In a heartbeat, he knew the driver was coming for them.

"Darby, look out!" Gage jutted out in front of her just as the SUV picked up speed as it came straight toward them. His momentum sent them backward, the bumper of the SUV clipping his leg as it roared past. He ignored the pain, scrambling up from where he'd practically squished Darby on the grass and reaching for her. "Hurry, we need to get out of here."

"D-did you see the driver?" She winced as he drew her upright.

"No." The sunlight was bright, and the glare had made it impossible to see the person behind the wheel with any sort of clarity.

But this was no accident. As he led Darby through a zigzag path through business parking lots and buildings, he kept a wary eye on the road in case the SUV came back for another run at them.

This was the fourth attempt to kill them. How many more attempts before Reyes succeeded?

CHAPTER SEVEN

Every muscle in Darby's body ached, between the hard landing on the ground beneath Gage and her zip line crash into the tree, she realized it was only the soles of her feet that didn't hurt.

Running with Gage in hiking boots changed that. They were comfortable for walking, but they were not designed for running.

Finally, Gage slowed to a walk, although he still appeared wary as he took in their surroundings. "Are you okay?"

"Yes." She'd only gotten a glimpse of the black SUV. "Was that the same car that ran you off the road?"

"I believe so, although I didn't get the license plate." He drew her toward a different restaurant. They'd already gone a good two miles from their previous location. "Let's grab something to eat."

"Eat?" Normally, she never turned down a meal, but after nearly being run down by a car, on the heels of everything else that had happened, she wasn't the least bit hungry.

"I could use some water, and the restroom. I should check out my leg."

"You were hit?" Darby hadn't realized. She slowed her pace to rake her gaze over him. "I don't see any blood."

"The bumper grazed me, that's all." He didn't look concerned. "We need to eat eventually, may as well grab something now."

He was right. She nodded in agreement.

They walked the rest of the way to the restaurant. Darby did her best to ignore the blister forming on her heel. Once again, Gage's quick reflexes had saved her life. It was strange, though, to go from shooting at them to trying to hit them with a car. Unless they were hit head-on at a high rate of speed, it's not likely they'd have died in the crash.

Injured enough to end up in the hospital? Oh yeah.

There was no way she could return to work in the morning. The stark thought filled her with dread. She didn't want to lose her job. Maybe Kent Jacobs would be understanding about her need to be off work.

And maybe he wouldn't.

The interior of the restaurant was cool against her hot and sweaty skin. Darby knew she probably looked awful, but she reminded herself she wasn't looking to impress Gage.

The man had already seen her at her worst. A memory she wasn't proud of.

The hostess led them to a booth. Darby dropped into her seat, grateful to take the pressure off her blisters. She didn't dare take her hiking boots off for fear of never getting them back on if her feet swelled even a little.

"You want to use the restroom first?" Gage asked.

She waved a hand. "Go. I'm not going to move for a while."

He disappeared into the restroom. Their server brought large glasses of water, which Darby gratefully drank, then rested the cool glass against her forehead.

They needed to go to the police with this latest incident. Not that she expected they'd do anything about it. Without a license plate number, and only a brief description, there wouldn't be a way to track the driver.

A wave of hopelessness washed over her. She hadn't felt this low since those first weeks in rehab, when every day loomed long and painful before her.

Pulling out her phone, she sent a quick text to Edith. *How's Leo?*

Great. Misses you.

Tears pricked Darby's eyes. *Not as much as I miss him.*

U need to talk?

Yes.

Gage returned to the booth, eyeing her curiously. Darby slowly rose to her aching feet. "My turn."

She disappeared into the bathroom. After using the facilities and washing up the best she could, she called Edith. "Hey, everything still going well?"

"We're fine, but Leo keeps asking about you."

The news wrenched her heart. She'd never spent this much time away from her son. And she was even more irritated that the forced separation was because of Reyes seeking revenge. "I'm sorry, but you'll need to stay where you are for a few more days. I'm trying to fix things here in town."

"That's fine, Darby, but you sound upset. Are you sure everything is all right?"

Nothing was all right, but Darby didn't say anything. She simply closed her eyes for a moment and rested against the wall. After a long moment, she managed to speak. "I'm sure." She strove to sound reassuring. "I just wanted to hear your voice."

"Let me put Leo on the phone." In the background, Darby could hear Edith talking to the little boy. "This is your mommy, can you say hi?"

"Hi," Leo dutifully repeated. "Mommy home?"

More tears threatened, and it was all Darby could do not to break down sobbing. "Soon, Leo. We'll all be home together very soon. Hug Oma, okay?"

"Okay."

The call disconnected. Darby stayed where she was, trying to pull herself together. Falling apart wasn't an option. Yes, she missed her son, more than she'd have imagined. But he and Edith were safe. That was all that mattered.

She straightened and returned to the booth. Their server came to refill their water glasses. "Are you ready to order?"

"Uh, sure." She'd only glimpsed at the menu. "Do you have a turkey wrap?"

"Yep. Want fries with that?"

"Yes, please. Thanks."

Gage ordered a buffalo chicken wrap. When they were alone, he asked, "You sure you're okay?"

"Fine." She couldn't drum up a smile. "Just missing Leo. And feeling like we're never going to escape Reyes."

"I understand how you feel. We need to call Detective Pride, let him know about the near miss on Wayland Avenue."

"Yeah, but what is he going to do about it?" She stared morosely at her water glass. "It's as if Reyes is toying with us. The squirrel and now this? What's his end game anyway?"

The moment the words were out of her mouth, she knew. "He wants us dead."

Gage leaned forward to grasp her hand. "I'm not going to let that happen."

She tightened her fingers around his. "The police will find him, won't they?"

"I hope so." Gage held her gaze. "We need to stay strong, Darby. Pray for God's guidance."

She opened her mouth to argue but hesitated. Maybe God was listening to Gage's prayers. It was difficult to deny they were still both relatively unharmed, aches and pains aside, despite the various attempts to hurt them.

"I'll leave that to you," she finally said. "I don't know how to pray."

Looking her straight in the eye while still holding her hand, he said, "Dear Lord, we ask You to keep us safe from harm and to guide us on Your path. Amen."

"Amen," she whispered, glancing self-consciously around the restaurant. No one was paying them any attention.

"All you need to do is speak from the heart, Darby," Gage said with a wry smile. "God doesn't have a strict format, He simply listens."

Listening wasn't going to help them find Reyes, but she didn't voice her skeptical thoughts aloud. Gage was entitled to his beliefs.

Just as she was entitled not to believe.

She couldn't help thinking back to those awful years with the Preacher. The way he'd ranted about their sins, hitting them for emphasis. How he'd focused on their need to repent.

How the fire had broken out, and every last one of the foster kids had managed to escape the burning cabin.

But not the Preacher or his wife.

God's doing? Probably not since she'd certainly helped fuel the fire. Not on purpose, but in retrospect, Darby knew the spilled moonshine the Preacher liked to drink may have played a role in how fast the fire had spread.

Moonshine she'd dumped over on purpose.

"Darby?"

Gage's voice drew her back to the present. He was still holding her hand, but their server stood impatiently, holding their plates.

"Sorry." She released Gage's hand and sat back to give the server room to set their plates on the table. When they had their respective wraps, the server left them alone again.

"Dear Lord, we thank You for this food we are about to eat. Amen."

She didn't respond. All this praying made her uncomfortable. "What's our next step?"

Gage took a bite of his wrap, his expression thoughtful. "We notify the detective, for sure. But I'm not sure what else we can do to find Reyes. He seems to have eyes on us, though, which is concerning."

She sent a furtive glance over her shoulder. "Yes, but how? I don't understand how Reyes knows every move we make."

"I wish I knew," Gage admitted. They both ate in silence for a moment, then he continued, "It's clear Reyes found you in the area and spent several days watching your routine. Maybe he did the same to me on the other side of town. Easy to see how he may have spied my damaged white truck at the Knotty Pine Motel, but these recent attempts?" He shook his head. "I honestly have no clue."

The news was hardly reassuring. Yet this wasn't Gage's

fault. She'd played a role in naming Reyes initially, along with turning on Gage.

And if she hadn't? Leo would have been born in jail and handed over to a foster family.

She'd made the best decision for Leo's sake at the time, and she would do it again in a heartbeat.

Only now her past had come back to haunt her. Gage too.

At least this time, Leo would be in good hands with Edith if something terrible happened to her. He wouldn't be shuttled off to strangers.

Yet the very possibility of never seeing her son again felt like a heavy rock sitting on her chest.

Making her wish there was a way to take away the pain.

GAGE DIDN'T LIKE the expression in Darby's eyes. A mixture of despair and hopelessness with an undertone of resignation. She picked at her food, which concerned him even more.

"How many hotels are located on this side of town?" Gage asked.

She furrowed her brow. "Lots, but they're all fairly full this time of the year. Why? You thinking of going from motel to motel showing Reyes's mug shot?"

"Why not?" Gage figured any action was better than doing nothing. And he wanted Darby to have hope they'd get through this.

She looked mildly interested. "We should split up, cover more ground that way."

"No." He wasn't budging on that point. "We stay together."

"Okay, but doing this is going to take a lot of time." She hesitated, then said, "I'll call in sick to work tomorrow."

"That's probably best." Remembering the impaled squirrel convinced him she wasn't safe to return to the adventure park. Even if she was working with other employees, Reyes wouldn't hesitate to take down anyone in his way.

Collateral damage.

Despite his own appetite taking a hike, Gage forced himself to finish his wrap. He glanced at his watch. "It's six o'clock now. I think we can probably hit a few motels yet tonight."

Darby perked up at his suggestion and took a healthy bite of her turkey wrap. "Okay, that works. Maybe we should do that first, before calling Detective Pride. We both know the hit-and-run incident isn't going to help nail Reyes. While finding someone who recognizes him would."

Her comment made him wonder if the detective had actually gone to the adventure park to talk to Steve Auckland personally. "I'd like to still leave the detective a message about the hit-and-run attempt. I did note that the vehicle was a Honda CRV."

"You did?" Darby's gaze looked at him with admiration. "I hardly got a look at it. I was too busy being flattened by you."

Her teasing tone made him smile. "I'm sorry about that, but I reacted instinctively. But this time, I also tried to pay attention to the type of vehicle coming at us." It was more than he'd been able to say about the rear-end collision.

That attempt had taken him completely by surprise.

"What if he's staying in a rental property?"

Darby's question gave him pause. "I guess it's possible,

but wouldn't someone do a background check before renting their place out?"

"I'm not sure. Maybe. But then again, Reyes could be using a fake ID."

"Yeah, something to hide his criminal record. But Auckland recognized him, so he couldn't have changed his appearance much. Fake name aside, we should be able to find someone who'll recognize him."

"I hope so." She munched a fry. "I want this thing over with, Gage. I need to spend time with my son. He's my anchor, and I'm feeling . . ." Her voice trailed off.

He knew how easy it was to relapse during times of stress. He reached over to grasp her hand again. "One more day, Darby. If we don't come up with something tomorrow, you should go and stay with Edith and your son. I'll find a way to pull Reyes out of hiding."

She clung to his hand for a long moment. "I don't like the idea of him coming after you either."

"Hey, we're smart. We'll find him." He injected a confidence he didn't feel into his tone. "And all that matters to me is that you and Leo are safe."

"Oh, Gage." She smiled wistfully. "Now that I've spent the past twenty-four hours with you, I can't imagine why I didn't tell you about Leo before now. Our son needs you. He needs a father figure. We have to find a way to find and arrest Reyes."

Her words warmed his heart. "We will," Gage assured her.

Failure wasn't an option. Especially now that he knew he had a son.

They finished their meal, Darby eating only half of her wrap, but he was relieved to see her appetite had seemed to return. For several moments, he'd feared she might spiral out of control.

Wasn't that why she'd voiced the desire to see Leo?

She waited until they were outside before asking, "Any idea where we should start?"

He took a moment to glance around the area. He hadn't paid much attention to their surroundings, other than to get far away from the scene of the hit-and-run. The bruise on his leg ached, but the muscle was only bruised, nothing more. "The hit-and-run happened about two miles from here. What if Reyes happened to stumble across us while returning to his motel? I say we check out a few places around here first."

She nodded. "That's a good idea. I was also thinking we should head back to the Knotty Pine at some point. That's where he took a shot at us, could be someone saw him prior to that. And our cars are still there too."

"Okay, we'll start here." He wished he had a map of the area so they didn't miss any of the motels. There was one located adjacent to the restaurant, so he turned in that direction. "I'll call for a rideshare after we hit this cluster of motels."

"You'll need to let me pay for something sooner or later," Darby pointed out. "At the rate we're using rideshares, you're bound to run out of cash."

He didn't like to admit she was right. It went against the grain to take her money, not just because he hadn't paid any child support during the first five years of Leo's life.

But because he found himself wanting to take care of her. To be her provider. Which was crazy since he'd barely gotten settled on his own two feet after his four-year stint behind bars.

"You can pay for breakfast tomorrow." He forced himself to make the concession.

"I'll hold you to that," she said in a mock threatening tone.

He grinned. It struck him that being partnered with Darby was nice. He'd kept to himself since reentering society, primarily because he'd been on probation and hadn't wanted to take any risks of being sent back. Over time, it became easier and cheaper to simply go home after work and eat in his studio apartment.

Most of the guys he worked with went out for drinks every Friday night. Gage had declined their offer so many times they'd stopped asking. But glancing at Darby now, it was all too easy to imagine spending Friday nights with her and Leo, maybe go to a movie or have a picnic.

Would Darby welcome that level of involvement in their lives? Or was she thinking of some sort of joint custody arrangement?

Plenty of time to work out the details later, once Reyes was safely behind bars. But Gage reverently hoped Darby would welcome him so they could spend time together as a family.

Gage left a message with Detective Pride about the hit-and-run. He figured they wouldn't hear back from him until the following morning. In the meantime, they began to make rounds to the motels. The first place they approached had a surly female clerk who squinted at them from bloodshot eyes. "Our clientele is private."

"I understand, but this man tried to kill us three times." Gage drilled the woman with a glare. "He's armed and dangerous, so if I were you, I'd avoid allowing him to hang around. You never know who he'll target next."

The clerk pursed her lips and took a closer look at the

two mug shots. He'd decided to show both Reyes and Archer, just in case they were working together on this.

"Neither of them look familiar," the clerk finally admitted. "But if they're so dangerous, why aren't the cops lookin' fer him?"

"They are. In fact, we spoke to Detective Pride earlier today." Gage took the two photos back. "Keep your eyes open. Thanks for your help."

Their next three stops were much of the same. Because they weren't cops, their questions about Reyes and Archer were greeted with suspicion or flat-out rudeness. While their reactions weren't unexpected, they were disheartening. Gage was quickly losing hope that their attempt to find Reyes was nothing more than a waste of time.

Reyes could be anywhere in the Knoxville area. Even, as Darby had pointed out, in a private home under an assumed name.

"Maybe we should head over to the Knotty Pine," Darby said with a sigh. "I'd like to make sure my car wasn't towed."

Both of their vehicles had likely been taken away, but he didn't say anything. It would be yet another added expense neither of them could afford.

Walking to each destination had taken time, and the sun was dipping down below the horizon by the time they'd reached the Knotty Pine. To his surprise, both of their vehicles were still in the lot.

"We need to drive our cars to a public parking spot," Darby murmured. "I'll need my car to get to and from work once this is over."

"Yeah." Gage thought about the places they'd passed along the way. "How about in the strip mall parking lot? They should be fine there overnight."

"Okay." She glanced at the lobby. "Let's check with the clerk first. Although it occurred to me that these places usually have more than one clerk on duty over a twenty-four-hour period. And we have no clue what time Reyes may have registered for a room." She grimaced. "We might have to hit all these same places in the morning."

"I had the same thought. But evenings and nights are the more likely timeframes to catch a glimpse of him. Daytime is when motel guests check out." He led the way into the lobby. There was a different clerk behind the desk than last time.

This guy was roughly Gage's own age of twenty-six, but he looked skinny and a bit malnourished. The former drug dealer recognized him as a potential user, but he kept his observations to himself.

Although, glancing at Darby, he could tell she'd noticed too. She subtly took the photos from him, shooing him back so she could take the lead.

He stayed a step behind her, determined to stay close in case this guy lashed out at her.

"Hey, you seen either of these two guys?" She showed the clerk the photos. "We're looking for—supplies, you know?"

"Yeah?" A flare of interest sparked in the kid's eyes. He leaned over to peer at the photographs. "This dude here." He tapped the picture of Archer with a dirty fingertip. "I think he's in room six."

"You sure?" Darby pressed. "I don't want to knock on the wrong door, stumble across the cops, if you know what I mean."

"Cops." The kid scowled. "They don't come here. Yeah, I'm positive he's in room six. Never seen the other dude, though."

"Okay, thanks." Darby folded the papers and tucked them into her pocket. "Don't let on to anyone that we were here. Wouldn't want him to get busted."

"I won't." The kid leaned forward. "What kind of stash does he have?"

"Whatever you need." She shrugged. "He's well connected."

"Wow." The kid looked as if he wanted to jump over the counter and head over to see what Archer was supplying.

"Hey, be cool," Darby cautioned. "Let us get to him first, then you should wait a while, just in case he's being watched."

"Yeah, okay." He looked deflated.

Gage drew her outside. "Nice work, let's call Detective Pride."

"Shouldn't we try to see him for ourselves first? Archer might not be in there."

Darby had a point, but knocking at the guy's door was a good way to get killed. But then he caught a glimpse of a man sliding behind the wheel of a black SUV. "That's him," he hissed.

Darby darted toward her car, using her key to unlock the doors, and climbed behind the wheel. Without hesitation, he jumped in beside her. She quickly backed out of the parking spot, spun around, and followed.

Gage silently prayed they weren't being led into a trap.

CHAPTER EIGHT

Darby gripped the steering wheel so tightly her fingers went numb. Her eyes were glued to the back of the SUV, trying to anticipate the driver's next move. At what seemed like the last minute, he turned right, so she quickly followed suit. "Can you get the license plate?"

"No, unfortunately, it's covered in mud."

She swallowed a wave of frustration. "But it's a Honda CRV, right? The same kind that almost hit us?"

"Yes. Careful, Darby, don't get too close," Gage cautioned. "He might recognize your car. For all we know, the reason Archer stayed at the Knotty Pine was to catch us returning to pick up our vehicles."

Gage made a good point. "I can't lose him." She continued following the path the SUV was taking. "He could lead us to Reyes."

"He might, or he could be heading to do some other sort of business," Gage countered. "Keep in mind, we're not armed, and we're not the police. No way are we going to confront either of these men."

Gage was right, Archer and Reyes were both armed and

dangerous. But just the fact that they found Archer filled her with hope that this nightmare would soon be over. She felt certain Archer was meeting up with Reyes. Once they were able to see both men, bonus points if they were doing something illegal, they could call in the cavalry.

The black SUV stopped at a red light. Darby tapped the brake, glad to have one vehicle between them. But the SUV abruptly turned right again, a loud horn blaring as the SUV driver cut off another car.

"He's getting away!" Feeling frantic, Darby noticed there was a driveway to her right, leading into a gas station. She yanked the wheel and pulled in. Cutting through the narrow openings between gas pumps, she pulled out onto the street the SUV had taken.

"I see him," Gage said encouragingly. "He's two cars up ahead."

She saw the SUV too. Or at least hoped so. Black SUVs were fairly common, and they were too far back to see the mud-covered license plate. Where on earth were the cops when you needed them? "Do you think he knows we're following him?" The idea filled her with dread. It was one thing to want Archer and Reyes arrested, but having them know they were onto them added a whole new level of danger.

What if Archer said something to Reyes? The two could be planning to capture her and Gage in a trap, box them in between their two vehicles to take another shot at them. The likelihood of missing from that short distance was slim to none.

"I'll call Pride again." Gage pulled up his phone. "If nothing else, the cops should pull that SUV over for having an illegible plate. Hopefully, they'll find drugs or a weapon, which puts him in violation of his parole."

That sounded promising. Darby didn't believe either of these men ever planned to go straight. She stayed two cars behind the black SUV as they continued down the street, heading out of the downtown area. It made her nervous because once they hit rural roads, they'd be more noticeable.

More vulnerable.

The SUV took an abrupt left turn. Gritting her teeth, Darby tried to follow, but the light turned red. Craning her neck, she could only watch as the SUV's taillights moved out of sight.

"The vehicle is heading east on Riverside Drive," Gage said into the phone. She wasn't sure if he was talking to the detective or to someone else at the police station. "It's a black Honda CRV with mud covering the license plate. We've identified the driver as Niles Archer, one of the suspects in the recent attempts to hurt us. There was a hit-and-run attempt by a black Honda CRV against us earlier today on Wayland Avenue."

By the time the light turned green, Darby knew the SUV was long gone. Still, she kept driving, hoping to catch up.

"Okay, thanks."

She glanced at Gage, who'd put his phone away. "Are they sending a squad?"

"Yeah, although I'm not sure what good that will do." He sounded dejected. "If we lost them, I'm sure Archer will find a way to elude the cops."

"He must have noticed me following him." She sighed and unclenched her fingers. "Otherwise, why would he suddenly turn like that?"

"I agree it's suspicious." Gage put a hand on her arm. "No point in trying to find him, I'm sure he's long gone."

While she appreciated Gage's support, she wasn't ready

to give up. Not when they'd gotten so close. "Just a little farther."

The car in front of her turned off, leaving nothing but wide open road stretching as far as the eye could see. Up ahead there was a curve in the road. Was the Honda still up ahead? There was no way to know for sure.

A shiver of apprehension slid down her spine, but she kept going.

"Darby, find a place to turn around." Gage tightened his grip on her arm. "I don't like that we're alone out here."

With reluctance, she eased off the gas, practically holding her breath as they rounded the bend. No black SUV was waiting there for them. Calmer now, she considered her options. "What about that place up ahead?" She gestured to the tavern located on the left side of the road.

"Sounds good."

Darby slowed even more, preparing for the turn off. Suddenly a vehicle came up fast behind her.

"Look out!" Gage shouted.

Darby instinctively yanked the wheel, trying to avoid a crash, but a second too late. Her head snapped back, her seat belt tightening painfully as the car smashed into them.

"Darby!" Gage's cry echoed as she fought to keep the car on the road. But it was a losing battle. Her vehicle was old, the tires worn, and she closed her eyes mere moments before they slid sideways off the shoulder and down into a ditch, hitting the ground with a bone-rattling thud. Pain bloomed in her face as the force of the impact deployed the airbags.

For long moments she couldn't hear anything but a strange hissing noise coming from the car engine. Lifting her head, she couldn't see anything past the shattered windshield. In that moment, she knew the car was a total loss.

"Darby? Are you okay?" Gage's voice sounded far away.

"Yes," she managed. Her entire body shimmered with pain, but she turned to look at him. He had a streak of blood across his face. "What about you?"

"We need to get out of here." She heard the grinding sound of plastic rubbing against plastic as he shoved his door open. She belatedly realized the car was sitting at an angle, her driver's side door pressed against the edge of the culvert. For a moment, she panicked at the idea of being trapped in the vehicle.

Gage managed to get out of the car, then reached in to offer her a hand. She struggled to release the latch on the seatbelt, then caught his hand in hers.

"I've got you," he promised, tugging her toward the opening.

Darby winced at the pain in her left ankle but heaved out of her seat, suddenly desperate to get out of the car.

With Gage's help, she was soon standing beside him. "Are you sure you're okay?"

"I think so."

"We need to hide in the trees, in case they come back." Gage took her hand and led her up the embankment to the wooded area.

Come back? She trembled with fear. She'd been sheltered by Gage during the hit-and-run attempt, but this total destruction of her car had badly rattled her.

They could have died. Especially if they hadn't been wearing their seatbelts.

She stumbled after Gage as they entered the woods. Ironically, she felt safer there, maybe because she often felt more at home in the wilderness than she did living in civilization. Remnants of those weeks she and Hailey had lived off the land after escaping the Preacher. Leaving the fire and the cabin the Preacher and Ruth hadn't been able to escape behind.

Old news, but the crash had provided some sort of weird flashback. For a moment she felt as if she were following Hailey through the dense brush, in a hurry to get away from the police who were searching for them.

"Let's rest here." Gage's voice brought her back to the present. "I'll call the police again."

It was disheartening to realize the police would likely never catch up to the Honda CRV. In fact, she couldn't honestly say what the make or model was of the car that hit them. Logically, she wanted to believe it was the same SUV, but she couldn't swear to it.

"They're going to get away, aren't they?"

Gage shot her a sympathetic look while he waited for the 911 operator to answer. He gave the crash location and requested an officer response.

Darby rested her forehead against the trunk of an Aspen tree, fighting through a wave of depression. Instead of getting a lead on Archer and Reyes, she was now without a vehicle. Another expense she couldn't afford.

Gage might believe in God, but she was pretty sure He had given up on her a long time ago.

If He existed at all.

GAGE WRAPPED his arms around Darby in an effort to ease her trembling. "It's okay. We're going to be okay."

"My car isn't," she whispered. "It's not worth much, so I doubt I'll be able to afford a replacement with the money the insurance pays me."

"I'm sorry about that." Gage tightened his hold on her. "We'll find a way to get through this, you'll see."

She didn't answer, but tears dampened his shirt. He felt terrible for her, but at the same time, he knew they were blessed to have survived with minor injuries. Things could be replaced.

People couldn't.

Especially Darby. He couldn't stand the idea of losing her. Not just because of Leo but because he'd come to care for her. A lot.

More than he should.

He cuddled her close, grateful God had been watching over them. "Please don't cry," he whispered. "We're alive, Darby, and that's the most important thing."

"I know." She sniffled loudly. She lifted her head, and in the darkness it was impossible to read her gaze. "But it makes me mad how Reyes and Archer have managed to get away with yet another attempt to kill us."

Anger was better than crying. "I know, but this will help the cops take our concern seriously."

"They better," she said tersely. "I don't want them to wait until we're both dead."

Through the darkness he could see the flashing lights of a police cruiser. "Okay, it's safe for us to go back to the road."

Darby drew in a deep breath and straightened, pulling out of his embrace. They made their way back toward the wrecked car as two officers approached holding up flashlights.

Gage instinctively lifted his arms to show he wasn't armed. "Officers? I'm Gage Killion, and this is Darby Walsh. I'm the one who called this in."

"Ma'am, please show us your hands."

Darby glanced back at him as she lifted her arms. "We're the victims here," she said curtly. "The guys you should be looking for are Niles Archer and Tyrone Reyes. Archer was last seen driving a black Honda CRV with mud covering his rear license plate."

"Yeah, we heard." The officer lowered his flashlight. "Please step closer so we can make sure you're not armed."

Gage knew it was standard procedure, but he could tell Darby was growing angry. "Easy," he whispered. "They're here to help."

"Then they should act like it," she snapped back.

"Act like what?" the officer asked.

"Nothing." Gage did his best to smooth things over. He was still on parole and didn't want to risk being sent back to prison. Stepping forward, he offered himself to be patted down. "I have nothing sharp in my pockets. There is folded paperwork in my right pocket. You'll find articles on the previous arrests of Niles Archer and Tyrone Reyes. We have reason to believe they're responsible for this crash."

The pat down didn't take long, and the officer quickly did the same to Darby. When the officer finished, she lowered her hands, planting them on her hips. "Did anyone find the black Honda CRV with muddy plates? We called that in well before we were hit from behind and sent into the ditch."

"I don't know." The officer who'd patted them down swept the beam of his flashlight over the interior of the vehicle, no doubt looking for drugs or weapons, before going around to check the rear bumper.

Gage joined him and pointed to the scuff marks where the vehicle had connected. "Looks like black paint."

"Yeah," the cop conceded. "Were you able to recognize the driver?"

"No, unfortunately, it was getting dark, and the headlights were too bright. The car came up fast, must have gained speed after the curve. We barely had time to react before we were hit."

Darby came over to stand beside them, her expression grim. Gage gave her a reassuring smile, hoping she'd calm down a bit. Antagonizing the cops wouldn't get them very far.

"Ma'am, did you see the driver?" The officer turned toward her.

"No. As Gage said, it all happened very fast. But we were on this road in the first place because we'd followed the black Honda. I can only imagine the driver pulled off somewhere and waited for us to go past so he could try to kill us."

"That's one theory," the officer said. "Or this could have been done by kids."

"No way." Gage was losing his grip on his own temper. "Call Detective Pride, I think you'll learn this is one of many incidents aimed at causing me and Darby harm. My truck was run off the road in a similar event such as this last Saturday. Darby's zip line cable was tampered with on Monday, and she crashed into a tree. Then we were targeted by gunfire at the Knotty Pine Motel, and just a few hours ago, we were nearly hit by a black Honda CRV while we were walking." He glared at the cop. "This is no coincidence. No kids out for a joyride. This is deadly serious, and we already know who is behind these attacks." He barely refrained from jabbing his index finger into the cop's chest. "All you have to do is find and arrest them."

This time, Darby reached out to put her hand on his arm.

The officers spoke in low tones to each other, then one

of them used his phone to make a call. Gage hoped he was talking to Detective Pride. His suspicion was confirmed when the officer returned. "We're going to drive you back to the station."

"What about my car?" Darby asked.

"A tow truck is on the way." The cop shook his head. "I'm sorry, but it looks to me like it's totaled."

"I know." Darby tossed the key onto the seat. "Doubt anyone will try to steal it."

Within minutes, Gage and Darby were sitting in the back of the patrol car for the second time in two days. So much had happened, and it grated on him to know the cops were no closer to finding Reyes or Archer.

Getting even one of them into custody would help. He had no doubt either Archer or Reyes would turn on the other if given the chance.

"Riding to the police station is getting old," Darby whispered.

"I know." Gage took her hand. "But we're in this together, Darby. All the way."

She glanced away, staring blindly out the window.

"What is it?" he asked.

"Just—nothing. So many different emotions are running through me, I can't even name them." She sounded exhausted, and he felt the same way.

"We'll head back to the motel as soon as possible."

She nodded but still didn't look at him. He wondered if she was thinking of going into hiding, meeting up with Leo and Edith. He couldn't blame her. It wasn't that long ago that he'd tried to talk her into doing just that.

But now the thought of her leaving filled him with dread. He worried she might decide to take off with Leo, find another place to live. It wasn't as if her job at the Great

Outdoor Adventure Park was something that would hold her in Knoxville.

Leo's friends, yes. But the boy was young enough that he could easily make new friends without a problem. Gage couldn't remember much of his life at age five. He doubted Leo would either.

The terms of his parole, on the other hand, demanded he stay in Knoxville. At least for the next three months. The thought of her leaving without him filled him with dread.

Detective Pride was waiting for them at the police station. He did not look happy to have been brought in this late. He wearily gestured toward the same interview room they'd sat in earlier that morning.

Gage followed Darby inside, and they sat across from the detective. Pride pulled out his notebook. "Okay, start at the beginning."

"Which beginning?" Gage asked. "I left you a message about the hit-and-run attempt on Wayland Avenue. The car that grazed me was a black Honda CRV. Same make and model as the vehicle we saw leaving the Knotty Pine Motel. I caught a good look at Niles Archer as he slid into the driver's seat. That's the car we followed through town and out onto Riverside Road. The same location where we were, once again, rear-ended and sent into the ditch."

"Why in the world did you follow the Honda in the first place?" Pride asked. "What were you thinking?"

"I was thinking we could keep an eye on the car until the police could get there," Darby answered. "The license plate was covered in mud; there was no way for us to get any other identifying information on it."

Pride drew in a deep breath. "You took a big risk, as you clearly learned after ending up in the ditch."

"You think?" Darby's tone was laced with sarcasm.

"Why haven't your cops found this vehicle yet anyway? Don't they pull over cars without proper plates?"

"They should, yes." Pride eyed her warily. "I'm sorry this happened to you. We have BOLOs out for both of the suspects you've identified, along with the CRV with muddy plates. I'm sure we'll find them very soon."

Gage didn't necessarily agree but kept his thoughts to himself. Darby was doing a good job of getting the point across without his help. "In the meantime, the attacks against us are escalating." He stared at the detective. "The very least you could do is let us know when you have one or both of these men in custody."

Pride nodded. "I can do that. Where are you staying?"

"A motel close by," Gage answered evasively. "But you need to send officers to the Knotty Pine, Archer was staying in room six before he left in the SUV."

"I have a squad on the way," Pride said.

"The clerk appears to be a drug user," Darby added. "You might be able to squeeze information from him. Reyes and Archer might be here to seek revenge against me and Gage, but that doesn't mean they aren't also involved in selling drugs again."

Gage suddenly frowned as an idea occurred to him. "When are they both due to meet with their respective parole officers?"

Pride looked surprised by the question. "Reyes doesn't have to report until Friday, but Archer is due tomorrow. We've put their respective parole officers on alert."

"And you'll have an officer there to grab Archer when he shows up, right?" Gage pressed. "For questioning at the very least."

"Let me worry about getting Archer and Reyes in for

questioning," Pride said, evading a direct response. "You two should focus on staying someplace safe for a while."

"Gee, that never would have occurred to me." Darby stood. "Thanks for your time, Detective."

Gage joined her as they left the police station. He could tell how disheartened she was by the whole ordeal. "I'll order a rideshare to get us back to the motel."

"That's fine." She rubbed her temple. "I need to call my boss. I was planning to call in sick tomorrow, but now that my car is trashed, I have no idea when I'll be able to return. I just hope he doesn't fire me for this."

"I'm sure he won't," Gage said, although he didn't know anything about the guy. "The zip lines are still down anyway, right? You're probably helping him out by taking time off."

She let out a harsh laugh but didn't say anything more as their rideshare pulled up. Gage waited for the driver, a female this time, to call his name before heading over.

When they reached their motel room, he unlocked the door. Darby swept past him, disappearing into the bathroom.

Gage sank onto the edge of the bed and lifted his heart in prayer. *Please, Lord, keep us safe from those trying to hurt us.*

He felt good about the possibility of getting Archer into custody when he shows up for his parole meeting. And if he didn't show, the cops would be looking for him anyway. Gage hoped he wouldn't take the risk.

When Darby emerged from the bathroom, she seemed better. "Sorry for being a pain at the police station."

He offered a crooked smile. "I didn't mind."

She blew out a breath. "I decided to just call in sick for tomorrow. There's no harm in taking this day by day." She hesitated, then added, "That's how I made it through rehab. One day at a time."

"I'm glad. And if they don't arrest Archer tomorrow, I'll drive you to meet up with Leo and Edith." It pained him to make the offer, but it was the right thing to do. "I can stay back to continue searching for them."

"Oh, Gage." To his horror, she looked as if she might cry again. "I was going to ask you to do that, but it's not fair to leave you here. We're in this together, right?"

The way she repeated his words back to him wrenched his heart. "Darby." His voice was husky with emotion. "What am I going to do with you?"

She smiled, and that was all he needed to pull her into his arms. This time, she went up on her tiptoes to kiss him. He welcomed her kiss, feasting on her sweet taste, knowing in that moment he would never muster the willpower he'd need to let her go.

CHAPTER NINE

Clinging to Gage's broad shoulders and soaking up his strength, Darby wished they could stay like this forever.

But, of course, they couldn't. This—attraction between them was heightened because of the danger surrounding them.

She reluctantly broke off from the kiss, burying her face in the hollow of Gage's shoulder. This felt good, felt right. But it could also be nothing more than an illusion. She had no idea what a healthy relationship entailed. Sure, she and Gage had loved each other, had created Leo, but that was when she was using drugs while Gage was selling them. What they'd shared six years ago was hardly normal.

What would it be like to see Gage on a daily basis, or even every couple of days, when he wanted to spend time with his son? Deep down, she accepted she was a bit of a thrill seeker. She needed something to help make her feel alive.

That need was one of the reasons she enjoyed her job at the adventure park.

"Darby? Are you sure you're okay?"

Gage's low husky voice sent a shiver skating down her spine. Being with him like this was dangerous. Which might be exactly why she'd kissed him.

Reluctantly, she pulled out of his arms. "Yes, sorry. I'm not sure what came over me."

"I'm not complaining," he said wryly. "But I don't want to rush you either. The fact is, now that we've reconnected, I don't want to let you go."

She felt certain Leo was a big reason he felt that way. And she couldn't blame him. He'd handled the news of his son better than she'd expected.

And Leo was first and foremost in her mind too.

She turned to face Gage. "I'm thinking of leaving town to stay with Edith and Leo."

A flicker of dismay crossed his green eyes, but he nodded slowly. "I understand. Are you leaving tonight or tomorrow?"

She blinked, surprised at his acquiescence. "Tomorrow. It's too late to head there tonight. He's sleeping by now anyway."

"Okay, how do you plan on getting there?" His gaze turned thoughtful. "I can call a rideshare for you if the location isn't too far away."

That he would offer to do such a thing made her determination waver. Gage had never been mean to her in the past, unlike Aaron Dukes. Gage had never raised his hand to her or put her down. But Gage had been on a mission to make money for them to live off of. This new version of him was even more difficult to resist. "I don't like leaving you to face this alone, Gage."

"I'll be fine. Leo needs you, and it's only right that you should be together." He rubbed the back of his neck. "We'll work out the details in the morning. For now, I should take my turn in the shower."

"Okay." She stepped back to give him space. Once she was alone, she changed into shorts and a T-shirt and crawled into bed. Every muscle in her body ached, but she did her best to ignore it. One thing about the pain was that it reminded her she was alive.

Thankfully, Gage was alive too. The image of her badly smashed car flashed in her mind. She pushed it away. That was a problem for another day. In fact, once she was reunited with Edith and Leo, she could begin the process of getting her life back to normal. She'd have to notify her insurance company and see what her options were to obtain an affordable vehicle.

Still, the idea of leaving Gage behind to deal with Reyes and Archer on his own didn't sit well. Gage was certainly capable, but he wasn't a cop.

Neither was she.

It was infuriating that the police hadn't found either Archer or Reyes. Scooping up Archer when he checked in with his parole officer was a strong possibility. But that didn't mean Archer would immediately roll over on Reyes.

Shutting down her whirling thoughts seemed an impossible task. She heard Gage emerge from the bathroom and make his way over to his bed. His being there helped her relax.

The next thing Darby knew sunlight streamed through the window. She pushed herself upright, shoving her tangled hair from her face. Gage's bed was empty, and she guessed he'd once again gotten up early to grab breakfast.

Despite the fact that it was her turn to pay for the meal.

Taking advantage of his absence, she used the bathroom and changed. The blisters on her heels from the two-mile run in her hiking boots had broken open. With a grimace, she pulled on fresh socks and the dreaded shoes.

Having blisters wasn't the end of the world. And based on what had transpired in the past twenty-four hours, that minor discomfort didn't even reach the top five on her list of concerns.

She paced the short length of the motel room, glancing frequently at her watch. It seemed as if Gage had been gone longer than usual. The restaurant was right next door. She told herself the place could be packed, even though it was only Wednesday.

Weekends would be busy, at least that was her experience at the adventure park.

Darby had left a message with Kent, using the car crash and loss of her vehicle for her reason for not coming into work. She hadn't heard back from him and wasn't sure if that was good or bad.

She couldn't afford to lose her job. Not when she already needed to find a way to pay for a replacement vehicle.

When the motel door opened, she spun around, her senses on alert. Gage looked surprised by the apprehension on her face, and she offered a wan smile. "Sorry, I guess I'm still on edge."

"Me too," he agreed, setting the bag of food on the small table. "I went to a different place for breakfast, going out of my way to make sure I wasn't followed."

"Thanks." It was incredible, really, that doing something as simple as picking up food could be dangerous. "Did the detective say what time Archer meets with his parole officer?"

"No." Gage shrugged and gestured to the food. "We should eat before it gets cold."

She came over to join him at the table. "Do you think he kept that a secret from us on purpose?"

"Maybe." Gage didn't smile, his expression serious. "But it's nothing you have to worry about. As soon as we finish breakfast, we'll get you out of here."

In the bright light of day, she was second-guessing her decision. But then Gage surprised her by reaching over to take her hand.

"Dear Lord, we thank You for this food we are about to eat. We ask that You continue to keep us safe, especially Edith and Leo. Amen."

She pulled her hand away from his without responding. "I'm surprised you still believe in God after all the attacks against us."

Gage eyed her thoughtfully. "God has kept us safe, Darby."

She shook her head. "If God was looking out for us, He should arrange for the police to grab Archer and Reyes."

"I didn't realize you were a glass-half-empty kind of girl."

She stared at him in surprise. "I'm not."

"You're looking at this backwards. God is looking out for us. He is the reason we're still alive and relatively unharmed."

It was disconcerting to see his point. "I'm not sure about that."

"I am, and if you open yourself to the possibility that God has helped each of us move beyond our past, I'm sure you'll see it too."

Was he right about that? Maybe. But she preferred to take responsibility for her own decisions. The good ones and the bad. It was something she learned in rehab.

While Gage had learned about God in prison.

"Darby, I know you've kept Leo's location a secret," Gage said, changing the subject as he unwrapped his breakfast sandwich. "But I'll need to know the general location in order to get you there."

"I'm sorry I didn't trust you with that information sooner." The past two days with Gage seemed like much longer. "Edith took him to a water park located in Asbury." She paused, then added, "That's where we went last month to celebrate Leo's fifth birthday."

"Really? I bet he had a blast." There was no denying the hint of wistfulness in his tone. "Leo knows how to swim?"

"Yes, I took him for lessons when he was three." She smiled at the memory. "He took to the water like a fish."

Gage nodded, and she could tell he was bothered by all the experiences with Leo that he'd missed. Sure, their son would celebrate more birthdays, but that didn't make up for the milestones he'd missed.

She batted down a flash of guilt. For one thing, she had no way of knowing Gage was out of jail or, more importantly, that he'd turned his life around.

If she had, she may have contacted him. Then again, to be honest, she hadn't given Gage much thought. Her focus had been on working, raising Leo, and staying sober. Revisiting the past had not been high on her list of priorities.

In fact, she'd done her best to forget about the multitude of mistakes she'd made. To this day, she regretted taking off with Aaron while Hailey was stuck in juvie. Those years with Aaron were the darkest of her life AP, what she silently referred to as After the Preacher.

Not that rehab had been a picnic.

"You've been a great mother to Leo," Gage said. "Thanks for taking care of our son."

"Why don't you stay with us at the water park?" The

offer popped out of her mouth, but she didn't regret it. In fact, she reached out to grasp Gage's arm. "Really, Gage, this way we can stick together while the police find and arrest Archer and Reyes."

He smiled and covered her hand with his. "I'd like nothing more than to spend time with you and Leo. But I also want the danger to be over. It's better if I stay here to make sure that happens."

"Please." She tightened her grip on his arm. "I'm worried about your safety."

"I appreciate that, Darby. But if we both disappear, these guys could simply lay low for a while, waiting for us to return. Who's to say they won't strike again?" He shook his head. "It's a risk I won't take. Not with your life. Or Leo's."

She held his gaze for a long moment before nodding in agreement. "If you're sure."

"Positive." He smiled reassuringly. "I'll rest easier knowing you and Leo are safe."

Releasing him, she focused on finishing her breakfast. It wouldn't take long for her to pack her things, and Asbury wasn't far.

She'd be with Leo and Edith well before lunchtime.

In spite of her desire to see her son, leaving Gage, even temporarily, felt as if she was leaving a part of herself behind.

GAGE TOLD himself Darby's leaving was for the best. He'd miss her like crazy but took heart that she'd be safer in Asbury with Leo and Edith than staying here with him.

He wished he could find a way to help her believe in God. Based on her statements, he sensed she was close. The

Preacher she'd lived with had done a number on her faith. And he could easily understand why it would be difficult for her to move beyond that experience.

Darby stood and cleaned up their wrappers. "Give me a minute to pack."

"Sure." He ignored the knot in his gut. "Take your time."

Using the map app on his phone, he estimated the distance to Asbury. Not too far, so taking a rideshare would work.

His phone rang as he was staring at it. Recognizing Detective Pride's number, he quickly answered. "Hello, Detective."

"Killion. I have good news for you."

Gage gestured for Darby to come over. "I'd like to put you on speaker."

Darby joined him. He placed the call on speaker and held the phone between them. "We could use some good news, Detective."

"We have Niles Archer in custody. And we have impounded his black Honda CRV, the license plate was covered with mud as you mentioned. There's also some damage to the front of the vehicle that indicates he's the one who crashed you into the ditch."

Darby sank into the chair, her gaze glued to his.

"We're very glad to hear that, Detective. Has he given you any information on the other incidents? Specifically the zip line cable?"

"No. Unfortunately, he's not talking other than to ask for his lawyer. And we didn't find a weapon in the SUV either."

Gage's hopes deflated like a balloon. "So Reyes is still armed and on the loose."

"A BOLO has been issued, and I'm confident we'll find him."

He truly hoped the detective was right about that. Glancing at Darby, he lifted a brow, silently asking if she had anything to add. She shook her head.

"Thanks again for the update, Detective," he said. "Please continue to keep us informed, especially once you find Reyes."

"Will do. Take care." Detective Pride disconnected from the call.

"They caught him," Darby repeated as if dazed. "I honestly didn't think they would."

He dropped down beside her. "Even better, it looks like they'll nail him for hitting us last night. That should be enough to send him back to jail."

"You think so?" Darby's gray eyes clung to his. "What if he claims it was an accident?"

"Still a hit-and-run, besides, he'll find it hard to explain why the license plate is full of mud when the rest of the vehicle isn't."

"Yeah." A small smile tugged at her mouth. "I hadn't thought of that."

"Well, the good news is that you can head to Asbury without worrying about things here. I'm sure it's only a matter of time until they find Reyes." He spoke confidently, even though he knew Tyrone Reyes was likely more adept at eluding the cops.

At least, he had been eight years ago when Gage had started working for him.

"I'm staying."

He frowned, thinking he misunderstood. "What are you talking about? Now that Archer is behind bars, you should feel even better about going to stay with Edith and Leo."

"One more day." Darby stood and faced him. "I called off work again today and happen to be off work tomorrow and Friday as I'm scheduled for the weekend."

He wasn't following her logic. "I still don't see why you'd want to stick around for another day."

"Don't you see? It was the two of us working together that helped get Archer behind bars. Maybe we can do the same with Reyes. Now that Reyes's assistant is out of reach, I suspect he's feeling rather desperate to put an end to this. To us."

He shook his head. "All the more reason for you to be far away from here. Better that Reyes comes after me."

She put a hand on his arm. "We're stronger together, Gage. And I'm encouraged by how quickly the cops caught Archer." She paused, then added, "If we can put an end to this here and now, you could join us at the water park. Spend some time getting to know Leo."

He wanted that so much, it was all he could do not to leave town right this minute. But Darby was right about one thing. The cops getting to Archer so quickly was encouraging. And it was clear they were taking the attacks against them seriously.

"Maybe just for a few hours," he agreed. "But if they don't have Reyes in custody by three this afternoon, I'm arranging for you to get to Asbury."

She lifted a brow. "You can't force me to do anything."

"True. But consider the fact that Reyes is due to report to his parole officer on Friday. There's a good chance this will all be over with by then."

"If he bothers to show up," Darby pointed out. "And based on what happened with Archer, I'm thinking he won't."

"Regardless, you were the one who wanted to be safe."

He was deeply touched that she'd volunteered to stick around even for a few hours. And he mentally cursed the weakness that allowed her to stay.

"Whatever." She waved her hand. "In the meantime, what's the plan? Do we go back to showing Reyes's mug shot to motel clerks?"

He hesitated. His initial plan, once she was safely in Asbury, had been to get his truck and drive around town in an effort to draw Reyes out of hiding.

Not something he wanted to attempt with Darby sitting in the passenger seat.

"Yeah, we could do that." It seemed the safer of the two options. "But I'd like to move my truck from the Knotty Pine, if it hasn't already been towed."

"We should have done that last night," Darby said with a frown. "I forgot all about it."

"We'd just gotten out of a serious car crash," he pointed out. "It will be fine. I'm hoping the motel staff are so distracted by the police investigation into Archer that they didn't have time to call for a tow."

"All right then, first stop the Knotty Pine." Her smile was strained. "Surely this trip will turn out better than the last one."

He glanced at his watch. There were two full hours before they needed to check out. "Why don't you stay here? I won't be long."

"No way." She slung her duffel bag over her shoulder. "We're better together."

"Is that our new slogan?" He took the duffel from her and shouldered both bags. "Have to say, I like it. 'Better Together' has a nice ring to it."

She laughed, and it was the first time in what seemed like forever that he'd heard the musical sound. Gage hoped that once Reyes was behind bars, he'd have lots of opportunities to hear her laugh.

Leo too.

Gage led the way to the lobby so they could check out. He wanted to be sure there were no charges placed on Darby's card. He insisted the clerk check the room out before they left, which he reluctantly did.

"By the way, you haven't seen this guy, have you?" Darby showed the clerk, who appeared to be in his early forties, Reyes's mug shot. "He's wanted by the police for trying to kill us."

"No." The clerk's eyes widened. "No offense, but I'm glad you're checking out."

Gage stifled a sigh. "None taken. But do yourself a favor, if you happen to see this guy, call the cops. It'll be safer for everyone."

"Yeah, okay." The clerk reached for the picture. "Can I make a copy?"

"Sure." They waited patiently for the guy to make a copy of the mug shot.

He returned a minute later. "I'll post this behind the desk."

"Good plan." Gage wished all the motel clerks they spoke with had done the same. Then again, some motels were probably catering to a criminal clientele. If not drugs, then prostitution.

Outside, dark clouds swirled overhead. Gage eyed them warily. He wasn't thrilled with the idea of being caught in a storm. He glanced at Darby. "Should we grab a rideshare?"

"No, let's walk." She lifted her gaze. "The clouds look like they're moving in from the west. I think there's time to get to the Knotty Pine before it hits."

"If you say so." It wasn't like they'd melt in the rain. But he felt more vulnerable out in the storm while Reyes was still on the loose. "This way," he gestured toward the left.

"Isn't the motel that way?" Darby asked with a frown.

"We're taking the scenic route." He fell into step beside her, keeping his body positioned between Darby and the road. Just in case Reyes showed up to mow them over.

"I was thinking about what you said about God."

He glanced at Darby in surprise. "Which part, exactly?"

A smile tugged at the corner of her mouth. "The part where you said God was watching over us. I never told you the details about what happened that night my foster siblings and I escaped the Preacher."

"I didn't want to pry, but I'll gladly listen." He shifted the weight of their bags and added, "There isn't anything you can tell me that will change how I feel about you."

She shot him a curious glance. "The Preacher and his wife died that night. I honestly have no idea what caused the fire initially, I assumed a log rolled out of the fireplace without being noticed. But I do know why the Preacher and his wife died that night."

His stomach clenched. "How?"

She blew out a breath. "I soon realized the Preacher was either drinking or taking drugs. His moods were so volatile, and his beatings grew worse as the day went on. I snooped around and found the Preacher's secret stash of moonshine. It was outside in a shed near the garden. I'm not sure why Sawyer didn't find it before me, or maybe he did and left it alone."

"Why Sawyer?" It was the first he'd heard of Sawyer. In the past, Darby had often mentioned her older foster sister Hailey.

"He was always working in the garden. Anyway, I

found the moonshine, sneaked it into the house, and dumped it on the floor beneath their bed."

Her confession wasn't at all what he'd expected. "So you're saying the fire broke out and grew in magnitude because of the moonshine?"

"Exactly." She looked almost relieved he'd understood. "It's not so much that I wanted them to die, but afterward, when we realized they must have died in the fire, I knew that I was responsible for their deaths." She shrugged. "I doubt God would approve of my actions."

"God forgives all sins, Darby. Besides, your intent wasn't to kill them in a fire. Your intent was to avoid another beating."

She grimaced. "The end result is still the same."

"You were how old? Twelve? Thirteen?"

"Twelve. Old enough to know better."

"No, Darby, you were a child being physically and psychologically abused. You didn't do anything wrong, and even if you did, I know for certain God forgives you. After all, I believe God has forgiven my sins, which are far worse."

She seemed to consider that as they made their roundabout way to the Knotty Pine. He could see the sign up ahead and quickened his pace, hoping his battered truck hadn't been towed away.

As they grew closer, Gage frowned. There were three police cars crammed into the small parking lot. Thankfully, his truck was still there, but he wasn't sure why there was such a strong police presence.

"What in the world is going on?" Darby asked.

"I'm not sure." He wasn't happy that his truck was blocked by one of the squads. Using his key fob, he unlocked the car and tossed their bags into the back seat.

"Do you see the police tape?" Darby's voice was low. "It's stretched across room number six."

"Hey, what are you doing here?" A cop strode toward them. "You'll need to leave, this is an active crime scene."

"What happened?" Darby asked.

The cop scowled. "You both need to leave. Now."

"This is my truck." Gage pointed to it. "If you can move the squad, we'll get out of your way."

"The truck stays until the crime scene has been cleared." The cop pulled out a notebook. "Although you showing up here saves me the trouble of tracking you down. I need your name and address."

Gage recited the information, keeping an eye on the motel room doorway. He caught a glimpse of a black body bag on a stretcher being rolled out of the room and being thrust into the back of a hearse. "Hey, who died?" God help him, he wanted the dead man to be Tyrone Reyes, putting an end to this nightmare once and for all.

"I can't talk to you about this." The cop pocketed his notebook.

Detective Pride emerged from the motel room. Gage sidestepped the cop and quickly called out to him. "Detective? What happened? Who died? Tyrone Reyes?"

Pride's expression was grim. "No, although he's my prime suspect, along with Archer."

Gage swallowed a stab of disappointment. "Then who?"

The detective hesitated, then said, "I need to talk to you both, anyway, so you may as well know. We found Ms. Walsh's co-worker, Steve Auckland, murdered."

CHAPTER TEN

Darby felt all the color leech from her face as the news hit hard. Steve was dead? Murdered?

Because he'd recognized Reyes, identifying him as one of his hikers? But how would Reyes have known about that?

She instinctively reached out to grasp Gage's arm, glancing warily over her shoulder. "Reyes has been watching us."

"We don't know that for sure," Gage protested.

"How else could he have known Steve recognized his mug shot?" She tightened her grip on Gage, feeling dizzy and sick to her stomach. "This is my fault. Steve is dead because I asked him about Reyes and Archer."

"We didn't kill him, Darby." Gage's low voice was meant to be reassuring, but she couldn't wrap her mind around the fact that Reyes must have been watching them. Through binoculars? Her stomach rolled at the possibility.

"Let's go inside the motel lobby," Detective Pride suggested. "I need you to explain to me again what transpired at the adventure park."

Gage slipped his arm around her waist. Grateful for his

support, she managed to remain on her weak knees as they followed the detective inside. The skinny clerk wasn't behind the desk this time, and she idly wondered what had happened to him. Hopefully, he wasn't anywhere near room six when the murder had taken place.

Considering the possible timing of Steve's death had her looking at Gage. "We followed Archer last night after he left the motel room. Do you think Steve was already dead by then?" The thought of Archer calmly walking away after killing someone only increased the swell of nausea in her stomach. "Or had Archer returned to kill him later?"

"For all we know, Reyes killed Steve and left him in Archer's room to make it look as if Archer did the deed," Gage countered. He turned toward the detective. "Can you at least tell us when you suspect the murder took place?"

"First, I need to hear from you about the last conversation you had with the deceased." Pride gestured to the sofa located across from a couple of chairs. "Please sit down."

Darby gratefully sank down beside Gage on the sofa. After exchanging a glance with Gage, she began. "We went to the adventure park yesterday to talk to the staff about whether or not they'd seen Reyes or Archer hanging around."

"Why?" Pride interrupted.

"Because I knew the zip line cable was tampered with, and the only way that I could have been targeted so specifically was if one of those men, Reyes or Archer, had been watching the place for a while. They'd have needed to understand our routine."

Pride scowled. "Showing photos of possible suspects is something better done by the police."

"We couldn't even get the police to admit the cable was

tampered with," Gage swiftly pointed out. "No one took our concerns seriously."

"You did, Detective," Darby interjected. "But that was well after the initial attempt to kill me. Sure, it might have been better for the police to question Steve, but wouldn't the end result have been the same?"

Pride sighed. "Okay, go on. You showed Steve the pictures of both Reyes and Archer."

"Actually, we showed them to both Teddy and Steve," she corrected. "Teddy was working the zip line cable with me when it failed. Teddy thought Reyes looked familiar, but he couldn't say anything definitive. Steve identified Reyes as being part of a hiking group last Friday. Three full days before the cable gave way on Monday."

"Did Steve notice anything off about Reyes?" Pride asked.

"Yes, he mentioned the guy was wearing sneakers rather than hiking boots and that he had a lot of tattoos. In Steve's opinion, Reyes didn't seem to be the type to go hiking."

"Anything specific about the tattoos?" Pride asked.

"No." She glanced at Gage, who shook his head. "I don't think he paid that much attention to the specifics of his tattoos. Reyes was just one guy in the group that Steve took up the Willow Point Trail."

The detective remained silent for a long moment.

"You should also know, Darby and I went up the trail after talking to Steve and Teddy," Gage said. "We found a squirrel impaled with sharp sticks attached to a tree."

"And you think Reyes did that when he hiked with Steve on Friday?" Pride asked.

"No, the carcass was too fresh for that." Darby glanced at Gage. "Now that Steve has been murdered, I think it's pretty clear Reyes was watching us. He saw us talk to Steve, then watched as we headed up the trail." She swallowed hard. "The squirrel must have been some sort of bizarre warning."

"If he was there, why didn't he shoot you?" Detective Pride didn't look impressed by the dead squirrel.

"I don't know." Darby looked down at her hand entwined with Gage's. "He certainly had the opportunity. It feels as if he's toying with us."

"Killing Steve may have been another warning," Gage said slowly. "I agree with Darby, I think Reyes was at the adventure park when we spoke to Teddy and Steve. I think he followed us and left the squirrel for us to find. I actually sensed someone watching us as we hiked down the trail to the park entrance."

Darby hadn't known that, but it explained why Gage had stayed directly behind her the entire time. "There is another possibility," she pointed out. "It could be Reyes watched from below, while Archer was positioned somewhere along the hiking trail."

"If they were both there yesterday, then I can't imagine why you two are alive and Auckland is dead." Detective Pride rubbed the back of his neck wearily. "It just doesn't make sense."

"There may not be much logic when it comes to Reyes wanting to exact his revenge," Gage said. "He's obviously stringing us along as a way to torture us."

"To keep us off balance, never knowing when and where he'll strike next," Darby added. A shiver rippled down her spine. "You need to find him, before he kills anyone else."

"Do you think Reyes killed Steve? Or Archer?" Gage asked.

The detective hesitated, then finally said, "We can't say

either way since we're still trying to track Archer's movements between the time you both saw him and the time he was arrested."

"What time was Steve killed?" Darby asked.

"We believe sometime between ten o'clock and two in the morning." Detective Pride rose to his feet. "I'm afraid that's all I can tell you. This is an ongoing homicide investigation."

It wasn't enough, but Darby was relieved to know that Steve hadn't been lying dead in the motel room when she and Gage had followed Archer.

Although she still felt the incredible weight of guilt for causing Steve to be targeted by Reyes in the first place. If only she and Gage hadn't gone over to ask about the two suspects. Maybe Steve would still be alive if they'd have just let the police handle the investigation.

"Don't, Darby." Gage spoke in a low voice as the detective left the lobby. "This isn't our fault."

"Isn't it?" She shook her head helplessly. "I painted a target on Steve's forehead."

"Either Reyes or Archer killed him, not us," Gage repeated firmly. "We are the victims here. And you know as well as I do the police wouldn't have gone to question the park staff members."

"They should have." Darby blew out a breath. "And I see that's what you're trying to say. That even if the police had questioned Teddy and Steve, Reyes would have still killed Steve."

"I believe so, yes." Gage stood and drew her up to stand beside him. "Let's see if they'll let me take my truck so we can get out of here."

She frowned. "I'm not sure us driving your truck is a good idea."

"I plan to leave it at the strip mall for a while." He pushed the door open for her. "I can probably avoid a tow by moving it."

His comment reminded her of the wreckage of her own car. A problem she still hadn't dealt with. As they crossed over to where Gage's white truck was parked, she couldn't help looking around in an attempt to spot Reyes.

Was Tyrone out there, watching their every move? Would he succeed in killing them?

She was torn about going to stay with Edith and Leo. Oh, she desperately wanted to, but just thinking of the possibility of Reyes following made her blood run cold.

Reyes had killed Steve. She had no doubt he'd just as brutally kill her son if given the opportunity.

Gage had somehow convinced the cop on duty to allow him to remove his truck from the motel parking lot. She imagined the scene of the crime was centered in the actual motel room itself.

"How are we going to stay safe?" She was hanging on to her control by a thread, the back of her neck crawling with fear. "Reyes could be watching us right this minute."

"We'll find a way." Gage opened the passenger side door for her. "And considering how many police officers are here at the motel, I doubt Reyes is anywhere close by."

She truly wanted to believe that. But she was beginning to think of Reyes as having eyes everywhere. She hung back from getting into the truck. "Reyes could very well have others working for him."

"Try not to panic." Gage's calm tone grated on her nerves. "Let's get away from here and then decide our next steps."

It wasn't easy to swallow her fear. With reluctance, she climbed into the truck. Gage slid behind the wheel, and soon they were on the road leading toward the strip mall.

Darby alternated between looking in the side mirror and turning to look directly behind them as they covered the short distance. Tense and expecting gunfire at any moment, she didn't relax even once they reached the parking area.

"I'll grab our bags," Gage said, pulling open the back door.

She huddled close to the truck, sweeping her gaze around the area. "Where can we go?"

"Let's try the coffee shop at the end of the mall," he suggested. "We can discuss our options there."

What options? From what Darby could tell, they didn't have any. Not if Reyes had others working for him, keeping an eye on them.

She felt certain they were sitting ducks, just waiting to be picked off. And the thought of never seeing Leo again nearly sent her to her knees.

"DARBY?" Gage hurried around the truck as she sagged against the side of the vehicle. "What's wrong?"

"I can't do this anymore." Her voice was a mere whisper. "I just can't. I'm so afraid I'll never see Leo again."

"Shh, it's okay. We'll get through this." He pulled her close. "Let's just get to the coffee shop. One step at a time, remember?"

He half carried Darby to the coffee shop. Thankfully, there was an open table, and he headed toward it. She collapsed into a chair and buried her face in her hands.

His heart went out to her. He sank down beside her and

put his arm around her shoulders. "Lord, please give us the strength we need to survive those who seek to harm us."

Darby sniffled and whispered, "Amen."

Surprised by her response, he tightened his hold. "We're going to get through this, Darby. God is watching over us."

"I hope He is," she managed in a hoarse voice. "Because I don't know what else to do."

"He is, Darby. He's always there for us." Her despair was heartbreaking. Gage felt certain their best course of action would be to find a way to sneak out of town to hide out with Leo and Edith.

Yet they needed a way to get away without being seen and followed. A trick he wasn't so sure they could pull off, unless they had help.

The woman behind the counter was giving him the stink-eye, likely because they'd taken a table without ordering anything. "I'll be right back with some coffee."

Darby drew in a ragged breath, lifted her head, and swiped away her tears. "Okay."

Encouraged by her rally, he headed over to buy coffee and a pastry. Darby always had a sweet tooth, and he hoped the pastry would help cheer her up.

Returning to the table, he was glad to note Darby looked better. "A pastry?" She lifted a brow. "You remembered."

"Yeah." He smiled. "I figured you deserved a treat."

"Thanks." She took the plastic knife and cut it in half. "We both deserve one."

They ate in silence for a moment. Gage had a plan but wasn't sure how Darby would feel about it. When their pastry was nothing but crumbs, he sipped his coffee, eyeing her over the rim of his cup. "We need help to get away from here."

She was instantly on alert, her gaze suspicious. "What kind of help?"

"I have a friend I think we can trust."

"Who?" She sat back in her seat. "Anyone I know?"

That almost made him laugh. "No. His name is James Donner, and he's the assistant pastor at my church."

Darby's expression turned skeptical. "Church? Really?"

"Yes, really. James is a good guy, welcomed me into the church despite my criminal record." He hesitated, then added, "We need to trust someone in order to escape Reyes."

She didn't respond for a long moment. "And James would take us where exactly?"

"To stay with Leo and Edith." He reached over to hold her hand. "You need to see your son, Darby. I know this has been incredibly hard for you to be away from him for the past few days."

"And you trust this James?"

"I do." He didn't hesitate. "With your life and Leo's. I didn't mention him sooner because I didn't want him to be in danger. But knowing about Steve's murder changes things. You were right about Reyes watching us. It's the only way he could have known about Steve recognizing his mug shot. We can't take my truck, it's too recognizable. And your car is demolished."

"What about the rideshare option?"

He nodded slowly. "We could try that, but I was thinking we'd take the rideshare to church, and then go with James from there. It adds a layer of protection."

"I don't know." She grimaced and looked away, staring through the window at the pedestrian traffic outside. "I don't like adding anyone else into this. Look at what happened to Steve."

"I don't think Reyes will kill James." Yet he could see she wasn't on board with the plan. "Okay, if you'd rather go directly to where Edith and Leo are, that's fine. We'll take a rideshare the entire way."

She bit her lip and shook her head. "I don't know what to do, Gage. I'm terrified of placing Edith and Leo in harm's way."

"I know. But maybe at this point being together is better than staying apart." It was clearly better for Darby's emotional health. "Maybe we ask James to pick us up here and take us to a specific location, maybe a halfway point. We can use a rideshare from there."

"That could work." She cradled her coffee to her chest as if chilled, despite the warm humid weather. She lifted her gaze to his. "My biggest concern is getting away from this coffee shop without being seen. We have to assume we were followed here from the motel. They must know your truck plate by now. And I feel certain that they'll see us the minute we leave, continuing to follow us wherever we go."

"Building codes require every restaurant to have a back door." He glanced around, spotting the narrow hallway leading to the restrooms. He stood and made his way down the short hall. Peering through the glass door, he could see there was a narrow road and another building. He quickly returned to the table. "Taking the back door out of here is our best option."

"You don't think Reyes has someone out front and out back?" She shivered. "I feel like he has spies everywhere."

He understood her paranoia. In fact, he shared it. There was no denying that Reyes was preying on them, taunting them.

Gage was hopeful that having James pick them up might confuse whoever was watching. He pulled out his phone. "Darby, I'm going to ask James to pick us up behind the coffee shop. We'll get away from here and have him drop us off somewhere safe."

She pressed her lips together but eventually nodded. "Okay."

Thankful to have a plan, he dialed the assistant pastor. James answered right away. "Gage, how are you?"

"I'm okay, but honestly, I've called because I need a favor."

"What can I do for you?"

He couldn't help but smile. He'd known James would help, and the guy's easy agreement helped put his mind at ease. "This is going to sound a little crazy, but I'm with a friend, and we need a ride. We're in East Knoxville now, and we would like to get to the nature preserve."

"No problem." James didn't hesitate. "Tell me exactly where you're currently located."

"We're on the west side of East Knoxville, at the Coffee Clutch located within the Maybury strip mall. But I'm going to ask you to meet us in the back of the strip mall rather than the front."

"Is there something going on that I need to know about?" James asked. Clearly, the directive to head to the back of the strip mall had raised a flag.

Gage didn't want to lie to the pastor. "My friend Darby and I are in danger from men who we knew years ago. I understand if that changes things for you. There have been several attempts to hurt us, and we're honestly just trying to stay alive."

"That sounds serious," James said. "You need to talk to the police."

"I promise you we have, several times," Gage assured him. "Detective Pride has my number, and I have his.

They've arrested one of the men involved, but another is still out there. And there's been a recent murder associated with this as well." The more he explained, the worse he felt about asking James for help. "You know, it's probably better if you don't come. We'll find another way out."

"I'll be there in forty-five minutes," James said firmly.

Gage locked eyes with Darby and slowly nodded. "Okay, thanks, James. I really appreciate your help."

"God put us on this earth to help each other out, especially in times of crisis," James reminded him. "And I know you would do the same for me."

"I would, yes. Thanks again, James." Gage disconnected from the call. "He'll be here in forty-five minutes."

"I hope we're doing the right thing." Darby sounded uncertain. "Bad enough Steve was murdered, I wouldn't want anything to happen to your friend."

"Reyes doesn't know about James or what vehicle he drives," Gage pointed out. "I'm sure James won't catch Reyes's attention until after we're gone."

She managed a wan smile. "Okay, I guess it's worth a try. Although I'm surprised James is willing to come after everything you told him."

"I feel bad dragging him into this," Gage admitted. "But I still think using James to escape without being noticed is our best option."

"What kind of car does he drive?" she asked.

"A dark green Jeep." Gage's cell phone rang, and he immediately assumed James was calling to say he'd changed his mind. But looking at the screen, he recognized Detective Pride's number. "Hello?"

"Gage, this is Detective Pride."

The muscles in his neck and shoulders knotted with tension. "I recognized your number. Is something wrong?"

"Yes, unfortunately. I'm calling to let you know that Niles Archer was found dead in his jail cell about two hours ago," Pride informed him. "Looks like suicide."

"Archer killed himself? Are you sure?" He noticed Darby startled at the news, spilling some of her coffee. Suicide didn't sound like something Archer would do. Not that he knew the guy all that well. Still, Archer was no stranger to being in jail, so why would being arrested push him into doing something so drastic?

"We won't know for sure until the autopsy has been completed, but it appears he used his prison clothing to fashion a noose, wrapping it around the bars in his cell and hanging himself." Pride paused, then added, "I'm sorry. We were hoping to get information about Reyes from him. We're still looking for Reyes, but we won't get any help from Archer."

"Yeah, thanks." Dazed, Gage disconnected from the phone. Learning Archer was dead only heightened the sense of danger.

And despite how the death was made to look like a suicide, Gage felt certain that Archer had been murdered, a deed ordered by Reyes. It was the best way to prevent Archer from telling the authorities what he knew.

In that moment, Gage felt certain Reyes wouldn't show up for his meeting with his parole officer on Friday. If the Knoxville police department didn't find and arrest Reyes soon, this nightmare could go on for a lot longer than the week he'd taken off work.

With sick certainty, he felt certain Reyes wouldn't stop until he and Darby were both dead.

CHAPTER ELEVEN

"I don't believe Archer killed himself," Darby murmured in a soft tone. "It's just—too convenient."

"You've got that right," Gage agreed. He drew his hands over his face in a tired gesture. "Way too convenient if you ask me."

She put a hand on his arm. Gage had held her together earlier, it was time for her to reciprocate. "Do you think he and Reyes had some sort of pact? Like if one of them got caught they'd kill themselves rather than squeal on the other?"

"It's possible." Gage covered her hand with his, and she couldn't deny the instant awareness that sprang between them at his touch. "Either that or Reyes bribed someone within the police department to kill Archer in a way to make it look like a suicide."

That theory made her swallow hard. Unfortunately, she'd seen enough while living on the streets to know that anything was possible. "If someone within the police department is helping Reyes, we really aren't safe here."

And it also explained how Reyes seemed to know their every move. "You don't think Detective Pride is involved?"

"No, he's been taking these threats seriously." Gage frowned. "But the cop I spoke to after the shooting, Officer Crow, was a total jerk. He kept harping on my past criminal record rather than questioning me about almost getting shot. I wouldn't be the least bit surprised to find out he was paid off by Reyes. Even his young partner seemed taken aback by Crow's attitude."

Darby didn't like the idea of a cop being bribed by Reyes. Yet she also knew that greed was a powerful motivator. "Maybe we should discuss this with the detective. He should know if Crow is really a dirty cop."

"Later, once we're out of the area." Gage's expression turned thoughtful. "If Crow is on the take, he could have easily run the plate to my truck and your car, providing that information to Reyes."

"I know." Depressing to think about it. "Explains how Archer knew I was behind him giving him time to double back and send us crashing into the ditch." It made her angry to think about her car being totaled because of a possible dirty cop.

"And if that's the case, we have to avoid your townhouse, Darby." Gage's expression was grim. "Reyes likely knows your address."

"Yours too," she reminded him. Although hearing this made her doubly thankful she'd convinced Edith to take Leo away for a few days.

Worse, there was no way they could return to the townhouse until Reyes had been arrested.

How much longer until the cops found him? Every cop should be aware of the BOLO.

Yet she felt sick realizing if Officer Crow found Reyes,

he wouldn't arrest him. No, he'd more than likely help the guy fly under the radar.

Gage blew out a deep sigh. "This is getting more complicated by the minute."

"Yeah. And I still think we need to tell the detective about our suspicions about Officer Crow. The cop could be sending Reyes information on where the police are searching for him. At that rate, they'll never find him."

"You make a good point." Gage pulled out his phone. "I'll let him know, even though I doubt he'll throw his fellow cop under the bus without hard proof."

Proof they didn't have.

Darby listened to Gage's side of the conversation with Detective Pride. "I know this is going to sound far-fetched, but I'm asking you to keep an open mind, Detective. I can't help but think that someone inside the police station might be feeding Reyes information. Someone like Officer Crow."

There was a long pause as Gage listened. She leaned closer, trying to hear Pride's thoughts, although the pained expression on Gage's face was a clue it wasn't going well.

"Yes, I know that accusing someone without proof is wrong. But I wanted you to know that not only was my truck followed, so was Darby's car. I can't imagine how Reyes or Archer would have been able to track our license plates. And it's just a theory. I'm sure the autopsy on Archer will provide some clarity on the possibility."

More silence as Gage listened. He caught her gaze, shook his head, and shrugged.

"Yes, I understand. Thanks for listening." He disconnected from the call. "Pride is not happy we're even considering law enforcement to be involved in something criminal. Told me in no uncertain terms to leave the investigating to him."

"I'm still glad you told him," she insisted. "Maybe as things play out he'll realize something is amiss."

"Maybe." Gage scowled. "In my experience, cops tend to stick together no matter what."

"I know." She drained her coffee. "Is there any possible way Reyes could know about your friendship with James?"

Gage carefully considered her question. "If Reyes had followed me for a while before rear-ending me, he'd know I go to church on Sundays and that I work long hours during the week. James and I play basketball at a local park on Saturday evenings. Reyes could have followed me there, but there are several guys on the team, I don't think he'd be able to identify James as a closer friend than the others."

She let out a silent sigh of relief. "That's good news. If Reyes doesn't know about James, and Officer Crow doesn't know about James, we should be safe getting out of here in his Jeep. Unless Reyes has someone watching the back side of the mall."

"We'll move so fast he won't have time to react," Gage assured her. "And James is only taking us to a new location. From there we'll take a rideshare to meet up with Edith and Leo. By the time he tries to follow us, we'll be long gone."

She nodded. It was a good plan, and frankly, she couldn't come up with anything better. She stared down at her empty coffee cup. "If we're going to be here for a while, we may as well get more coffee." She stood. "Give me a minute to use the restroom and I'll buy us a second cup."

"I can get it," Gage protested.

"You haven't let me pay for anything," she admonished him. "Coffee is on me."

He didn't look happy, but he didn't argue. She knew he was still feeling guilty about all the years he hadn't paid child support. Ridiculous, really, since she hadn't even told him about Leo. Had actually never planned to.

Looking back on that, she experienced a flash of guilt. What if Gage hadn't found her working at the Great Outdoor Adventure Park? She would never have tried to find him.

The way she hadn't tried very hard to find her foster siblings.

She finished in the bathroom, shook off the regret, and tried to stay focused on what was important.

Sneaking out of East Knoxville and getting to Leo and Edith without being followed, in order to keep them safe.

Life without Leo was meaningless.

GAGE REPLAYED his brief conversation with Detective Pride in his mind as Darby bought two large coffees and another pastry. The detective had not been happy and accused him of sullying the reputation of a good cop.

Officer Crow hadn't come across to him as a good cop, but Gage knew his opinion didn't mean squat. Not to those who wore the uniform and carried a badge.

He tried to shake off the detective's anger. Maybe Darby was right, that at some point the detective would come around to their way of thinking.

Or it could be that Crow was innocent and he and Darby were the ones grasping at straws.

He'd called in favors to find Darby, recognizing her photo as one of the employees at the Great Outdoor Adventure Park website.

But he had no idea how Reyes or Archer had found him. His name wasn't anywhere on the construction company's website. He didn't do any social media. The only person he'd even considered getting in touch with was Darby, but he'd put off searching for her until the day he'd been rear-ended by the black SUV.

Gage firmly believed God had brought him to Darby. And maybe God wanted him and Darby to put their past to rest once and for all.

"I'm pretty sure you still take your coffee black, right?" Darby asked, setting his cup down. "If not, let me know."

"I do, thanks." He glanced at his watch. "We still have thirty minutes before James will be here. Do you want to call Edith and Leo?"

"No, I'd rather wait until we get to the nature preserve." She shrugged. "Just in case something happens and we're forced to take a detour. I wouldn't want Edith to wait for us unnecessarily."

"I understand." He hoped they wouldn't be delayed, but she was right to be prepared for the worst. He stood. "My turn to use the restroom."

He followed the short hallway to the bathroom facilities. The hallway ended with a door leading outside. To the right was another door, likely leading to the kitchen area. The coffee shop wasn't large and only offered baked goods, but there still had to be a decent-sized kitchen back there.

Going up to the glass doorway, he peered out at the area behind the strip mall. He took his time, looking carefully for any possible hiding spots where Reyes could have someone waiting and watching. But he didn't see anything remotely suspicious.

The corner of a green dumpster was visible to the left. Maybe all the shops located within the strip mall used the same dumpster. Or there could be more. Either way, he was relieved that James could easily get into the alley to pick them up without a problem.

Getting Darby someplace safe was his top priority. Well, that and meeting his son. He'd tried not to focus on that part, knowing he'd be overwhelmed with emotion.

Safety first, then he could worry about Leo's reaction to meeting his father for the first time.

His father.

A niggle of doubt crept in. What did he know about being a father? His dad had left when Gage was ten, and the guy hadn't been around much in the first place anyway. His mother remarried two years later, and that's when the physical abuse began. Not bad at first, but mostly because Gage had been scrawny until he'd hit puberty. Once he grew taller and filled out, his stepfather became even more violent.

Gage knew it was either fight back to the point of almost killing the guy or leave. He chose the latter.

The only positive male role model Gage had was Pastor Davies. His friend James was his age, and he was more like a brother than a father. Pastor Davies had a wife, but no kids that he knew of. James was still single.

Gage had no idea how to be a father. But he was willing to try. Because Leo deserved that much.

And more.

So did Darby.

After using the bathroom, Gage returned to the table. Before he could take a sip of his coffee, his phone rang. Recognizing James's number, his spirits sank. "Hey, James. Did you change your mind?"

"No, why would I do that?" James sounded slightly annoyed. "I was able to leave right away, so I'm only five minutes out. Figured you'd need time to get outside."

"Five minutes is perfect." He met Darby's eye and gave her a thumbs-up. "We'll be waiting. The doorway leading out of the coffee shop is near a large green dumpster."

"Got it. See you soon." James disconnected from the call.

"Finish up your half of the pastry." Darby offered a smile. "I'm glad we're getting out of here."

"Me too." He ate the pastry and finished his coffee. The runaway in him wouldn't allow him to waste food for any reason. He shouldered their bags, then moved toward the bathrooms. "Stay behind me," he said in a low voice.

"Okay." Darby lightly gripped the hem of his T-shirt.

He peered through the glass door, waiting for James to arrive. It seemed to take longer than five minutes, but the Jeep pulled in and stopped directly in front of the door.

"Let's go." Gage pushed through the doorway, yanked open the back door of the Jeep, and tossed the bags in. He waited for Darby to climb in, then shut the door and ran around to the passenger side. He was braced for the worst, but nothing happened.

"Darby, put your head down," Gage directed as he did the same. James drove through the alley to the next corner, then turned right.

No one spoke for several long minutes as James negotiated the Jeep through traffic.

"Okay, I think you can both sit up now." James glanced at him. "You really are in danger."

"Yeah." Gage offered a crooked smile. "Thanks for being willing to help in spite of that." He half turned in his seat. "James, I want you to meet a friend of mine, Darby Walsh. Darby, this is James Donner, he's the assistant pastor at church."

"Nice to meet you," Darby said. "I echo what Gage said.

We appreciate you helping us escape the city without being followed."

"You've been followed?" James asked with a frown.

Darby let out a harsh laugh. "Oh, we've been worse than that. Gage, tell him."

Gage went through the story as briefly as he could. But when he got to the part about the gunfire outside the Knotty Pine Motel, James put up a hand.

"You're saying these guys rear-ended your truck, caused Darby to fall off the zip line, and shot at you?" His tone was incredulous.

"They ran us off the road too, totaled my car," Darby added. Her expression turned sorrowful. "And they killed one of my co-workers at the park, just because he spoke to us."

James whistled. "If I was hearing this from anyone else, I wouldn't believe it."

"Trust me, I still have trouble believing it." Gage sighed. "And Detective Pride is aware of everything. There's a BOLO out on Tyrone Reyes, but so far he hasn't been picked up."

"You can both come back to my place," James offered. "I'm happy to have you until the police arrest this guy."

"That's very kind, but Darby wants to be reunited with her son." Gage glanced at her, silently asking how much she wanted James to know.

"Leo is five, and he's at a local water park with Edith, a woman who kind of adopted us after I got out of rehab," Darby explained. He could see her looking at James through the rearview mirror. "Gage and I were together six years ago. Leo is his son too."

"Wow." James sent him a questioning glance. "I guess congratulations are in order."

"We have been blessed with a son, so yes, it's a good thing." He could see the wheels spinning in James's mind. "Darby and I have a lot to discuss, but first and foremost, Leo and Edith need to be kept safe."

"Understood." James nodded. "You asked me to take you to the nature preserve, but I can easily take you all the way to the water park."

Gage hesitated, glancing again at Darby. "I know you would do that, James, but we're being extra cautious. Too many things have happened in the past few days. It's probably best for us to grab a rideshare from the nature preserve."

"Okay." Thankfully, James didn't look put out by his request. "But, Gage, I would like you to keep me in the loop. I would hate to hear about something bad happening to you or to Darby from a newspaper."

"I will." Gage hesitated, then added, "I hope you don't mind keeping this trip to yourself. At least until Reyes is caught."

"Absolutely." James once again caught Darby's gaze in the rearview mirror. "I hope you bring Leo to church once all this is over."

"Ah, maybe." Darby flushed, and Gage knew she was thinking about her time with the Preacher. "We'll see."

"Or if you have a church you attend, I'm happy to join you for services," James countered.

"We'll find a way for you to meet Leo," Gage promised. "And we truly appreciate your help today."

James nodded and thankfully let the subject of church services go. Darby was only just beginning her relationship with God. He didn't want to do anything that would send her farther away from Him.

Of course, he'd love nothing more than to have her and

Leo, Edith too if she wanted, attend church services with him. But he was willing to be patient.

To wait as long as necessary to win Darby over.

Gage noticed James was glancing frequently in his rearview mirror. "What's wrong?"

"I've noticed there's a black pickup truck that has been behind us since we left the strip mall. Any chance he's one of the men trying to harm you?"

Gage resisted the urge to turn and stare out the back window. "Maybe, but not likely. But I'd rather be safe than sorry. Turn and head in the opposite direction, see if the truck follows. Oh, and, Darby, don't turn to look. Let's not draw attention to ourselves or let on that we've seen the truck."

"It can't possibly be Reyes," Darby said in a hoarse voice. "We stayed crouched down in our seats. How could he have recognized the Jeep enough to follow?"

It was a good question. "You may have been right when you mentioned Reyes has others working for him. Could be he had someone watching the road behind the strip mall with instructions to follow anyone going through there. I have a sense that road only sees a certain type of traffic, like trucks delivering food and supplies or garbage pickup."

James went into a left turn lane, but instead of turning left, he executed a U-turn. The maneuver gave Gage a moment to look at the driver of the black truck. The guy wore a baseball hat, but from the brief glimpse, he didn't think the driver was Reyes.

"I didn't get a good look, but the guy looked too skinny to be Reyes," Darby said.

"Yeah, but it could be someone Reyes has hired," Gage felt compelled to point out.

"Definitely, because the black truck just pulled the same U-turn." James sounded grim. "Now what?"

"Head back to East Knoxville straight to the police station." Gage hated knowing he'd put his friend in danger. "Do you know where it is?"

"Not offhand, sorry."

"Turn right at the next light." Gage continued to give James directions to the police station. James also moved from one lane to the next in an attempt to throw off the black truck.

Unfortunately, the truck kept pace with them.

"Gage?" Fear underlined Darby's tone. "What if he's calling Reyes? They could trap us here."

"We'll get to the police station before that happens," he said reassuringly.

"God will guide us," James added.

Darby's expression was dismayed, but then she whispered, "God, please keep us all safe."

Gage took heart from hearing Darby's prayer, the first one she'd said out loud.

And added one of his own too.

CHAPTER TWELVE

Darby twisted her fingers in her lap and tried not to panic. When James had made that sudden U-turn, she'd quickly turned to get a look at the driver of the black truck. The image was mostly a blur, although she had been relieved to register a rather skinny man behind the wheel rather than someone thick around the neck like Reyes.

Gage was right in thinking Reyes must have hired someone to watch the rear side of the mall. A sense of despair hit hard. It seemed that no matter what they tried to do to get away, Reyes and his men were one step ahead of them.

God, please, keep us safe.

For the first time in her life, she'd sought solace in prayer. There was no denying the sense of calm that washed over her when she'd uttered those words, but at the same time, she wasn't completely certain God would listen to her.

All the things she'd done. The mistakes she'd made. The horrors of the Preacher's cabin, and the way she'd spilled moonshine all over the floor beneath the Preacher's bed. Being with Aaron, then Gage. Doing drugs. The memories hurt and made her want to hide her face in shame.

The only really good thing she'd done in her life was get clean and have Leo. Her son was the center of her world. And it occurred to her that the best way to get away from Reyes was to simply pack up and move somewhere else.

Far, far away.

With Gage? She shied away from answering that question.

"Take another left at the light, the police station is about a mile down the road," Gage instructed.

"The truck is falling back," James said.

"He probably knows the police station is our ultimate destination." Gage turned to look at her. "Are you okay?"

She untwisted her fingers with an effort. "Yes. But now what are we going to do? Reyes's accomplice knows James's Jeep. And your truck." She fought a wave of hopelessness. "A rideshare?"

"Let's talk to Detective Pride first," Gage said. "Did anyone glimpse the license plate number?"

"I caught a glimpse of the first three numbers 562, when we passed it after the U-turn," she said. "But I can't tell you much else."

James glanced at Gage. "I think it's a Ford truck, but I couldn't swear to it."

"I thought it was a Ford too, and even a partial plate is better than nothing," Gage said. "Nice job, Darby. You helped a lot."

She wished she could share his optimism. "What good is a partial plate? Any idea how many black Ford trucks there are in the entire state of Tennessee?"

"The first three digits will narrow that list significantly,"

Gage assured her. "And maybe we can get the police to drop us off in a neutral location."

"I feel as if I've failed you," James said. "I'm sorry."

"You didn't fail us," Darby protested. "I think it's more the other way around. We shouldn't have asked for your help, considering the danger."

"Darby is right." Gage sighed as James pulled to a stop in front of the police station. "I'm sorry we put you in harm's way."

"I offered, remember?" James reached out and touched Gage's arm. "I'm worried about you and Darby. These guys seem very determined to find you."

"Once we get out of town, we should be fine," Gage said. "Thanks again for your help."

Darby pushed open her door and slid out of the Jeep. She reached for the bags, but Gage grabbed them before she could.

Together they went inside the police station. Gage asked to speak to Detective Pride, only to be told the guy wasn't in.

"Now what?" she asked. It was difficult for her to keep winging it like this. She liked having a plan. And right now it seemed as if their only plan was to hide out in the police station, and they wouldn't be able to stick around for long.

"I'll call the detective." Gage pulled out his phone, but it appeared the detective didn't answer because he left a message. "Detective Pride, this is Gage Killion. We were followed by a black Ford truck, three digits on the license plate are 562. We believe the driver was working for Reyes. Please call me as soon as possible."

"Now what?" she repeated. "That woman behind the desk is glaring at us."

Gage blew out a heavy breath. "We'll walk to the closest

restaurant and wait for Pride to call us back."

As plans went, it wasn't impressive. But she could see some logic in staying close to the police station. She brightened. "Hey, maybe we can find a restaurant where a bunch of cops hang out."

"Good idea," Gage agreed. He turned toward the woman who was still glaring at them. "Where is the nearest restaurant?"

The female officer pursed her lips for a moment. "The 799 is two blocks south of here."

"That's the name of the place? The 799?"

"Yes. Former cop owns the place. That was his badge number."

"Perfect, thanks." Gage grinned and caught her hand. "Hear that? Let's go eat with the police."

Walking outside the police station made her feel vulnerable. Gage positioned himself between her and the street, but she found that upsetting too. She didn't want anything to happen to Gage. He'd already saved her life several times; she worried about Reyes getting to him.

These past few days with Gage had made her realize how much she liked him.

How much she cared about him.

"There's the sign," Gage murmured. "We're almost there."

She nodded. "I think you're right about Reyes and his accomplice leaving us alone this close to the police station. I only hope Detective Pride calls you back soon. It seems like the only way we'll get out of here is with help from law enforcement."

"Yeah." Gage swept his gaze around, no doubt searching for the black Ford truck. Yet they had no idea what vehicle Reyes might be driving.

She followed Gage's glance with one of her own, knowing Reyes could be anywhere.

The 799 was busy. Many of the customers were cops in uniform, but there were just as many who weren't. Darby relaxed a bit, realizing they wouldn't stick out too badly amongst the group.

A sweet girl who looked about seventeen or eighteen led them to a booth near a window. Gage slid into the seat that faced the doorway, setting their bags on the floor at his feet.

"Your server will be right with you," the young girl said.

"I can't drink any more coffee," Darby said wryly. "My heart already feels like it's racing. And I'm not hungry either."

"We have to order something." Gage drew his plastic menu closer. "Maybe we can split a burger and fries?"

"That's fine." She didn't really care what he ordered. Her stomach was still in knots over their near miss with the Ford truck. "How long do you think we'll have to stay here?"

"Only as long as it takes for Pride to call me back." Gage reached over to take her hand. "I know this has been a long morning, but keep in mind, we're still alive and well. Leo and Edith are still safe. And we're going to find a way out of town to meet up with Leo and Edith."

"Promise?" Her tone was wistful, even though she knew he couldn't promise her anything.

"I promise to do everything I can to make that happen."

"I know. I trust you, Gage."

He smiled, but then leaned back when their server arrived. Darby sipped her ice water as Gage placed their order. "We're going to share if that's okay."

The server eyed them warily. "That's fine."

Again, sharing a meal reminded her of those first few

years after escaping the preacher. How many times did Hailey manage to scrape a few dollars together to buy a fast-food burger that they'd have to split in half?

Too many times to count.

"Hey, what's wrong?"

Her expression must have reflected her thoughts. "Oh, nothing. I was just thinking of my foster siblings, especially my sister Hailey. I haven't seen any of them in years because I never took the time to try and find them."

"Being a single mother and working full time probably didn't give you much free time," Gage pointed out.

"No, but I also didn't make it a priority." She took another sip of her water. "Especially Hailey. I took off with Aaron when she ended up in juvie, and I haven't seen her since." She grimaced. "Leaving her to go with Aaron was one of the biggest mistakes of my life."

"I can see where you'd think so," Gage agreed. "But, Darby, your leaving with Aaron was what brought us together. And without us being together, you wouldn't have Leo."

She slowly nodded. "True."

"Don't spend all your time looking backward, trying to erase the mistakes you made. What you need to remember is that every step you took, even the wrong ones, brought you here. To today. To the life you've made with Leo and Edith." He hesitated, then added, "And with me. I'm grateful we've been able to beat the past, Darby. Both of us are in a much better place now."

"For all the good it's doing, with Reyes trying to kill us."

"I know. We've spoken before about how hard it is to understand God's plan for us, but have faith, Darby. Things will get better. All of this"—he waved a hand—"will work out exactly the way it should."

"I'll try." It was the best she could offer. He made a good point, she couldn't regret that time with Aaron when leaving him after being smacked around for the umpteenth time was how she'd ended up with Gage.

A relationship that had created Leo.

She stared at their clasped hands for a long moment. Gage was right. She couldn't keep living in the past.

Staying focused on the future was more important. But with Reyes and whoever the skinny guy was driving the black truck following them, she was having a difficult time thinking about what her future would hold.

At this point, she didn't know whether or not she and Leo and Gage would have a future at all.

GAGE DIDN'T KNOW what else he could say to lift Darby's spirits. He shared her concerns, but he wasn't giving up.

Not by a long shot.

Raking his gaze over the officers seated within the restaurant, he spied Officer Crow. For a brief moment, their gazes locked, and even from this distance, Gage could see the smirk when Crow recognized him.

Their server arrived with their food, breaking the moment. Gage took a moment to send up a silent prayer of thanks, before cutting the burger in half and offering it to Darby.

"Try to eat something," he encouraged. "We don't know when we'll have the chance to eat again."

"I guess." She halfheartedly picked at a fry.

"Don't look now, but Officer Crow is sitting catty-corner from us with his same young partner who questioned you." Gage took a bite of the juicy burger and nodded in satisfaction. "This is really good."

Darby ate her fry, then reluctantly picked up the other half of his burger. "Did he see you?"

"Yeah." Gage kept an eye on the guy through his peripheral vision. A few minutes later, Crow and his young partner rose and left the restaurant.

"We were probably wrong about him," Darby said. "No wonder Detective Pride was annoyed. I think it's clear that the skinny guy driving the truck is the accomplice. He's probably been helping Reyes all along. Between skinny guy and Archer, Reyes could easily have kept tabs on our vehicles."

"I still don't trust Crow as far as I can throw him." Gage struggled to shake off his bad attitude. Crow wasn't the first cop who'd treated him poorly because of his criminal record, and he likely wouldn't be the last.

Time to move on.

His phone rang as they were finishing their meal. Gage pounced on it, relieved to recognize Pride's number. "Detective? Thank you so much for calling us back."

"You're absolutely certain the black Ford was following you?" Heavy doubt laced the detective's tone.

"Yes, I'm sure. We made a U-turn at a left turn light, and the truck did the same thing."

There was a moment of silence. "I ran the plate and found an owner of a Ford truck who recently reported his license plate was stolen. The stolen plate number is 5624TJ."

"Stolen." A stab of disappointment hit hard. "That figures."

"Where are you?" Pride asked.

"We're at the 799," Gage informed him. "We wanted to

be near other police officers in an effort to avoid being targeted again."

"That was smart," Pride admitted.

"Detective, we need your help to get out of town. Reyes and his accomplice are clearly watching our every move. A friend of mine tried to help, but we were still followed." Gage paused, looking at Darby, then added, "Please."

Another moment of silence, and Gage prayed the detective would find a way to help them escape.

They were quickly running out of options.

"I'll be there in twenty minutes," Pride finally said.

Gage sighed in relief and smiled encouragingly at Darby. "Any chance I could convince you to meet us at the police station? Maybe there's a back door you could take us through? We easily could have been followed here to the 799."

"Yeah, fine. We'll meet at the station in twenty minutes." The detective sounded put out, but Gage didn't care.

"Thank you very much." He disconnected from the call. "Twenty minutes. I think that gives us time to share a dessert."

For the first time in what seemed like hours, Darby smiled. "Anything but apple pie."

He groaned. "But that's my favorite."

"I prefer French silk," she countered. "In case you've forgotten."

He signaled for the server to return. Of course he hadn't forgotten, he'd only wanted to tease her.

"You really think Detective Pride can sneak us out of here?" Darby asked.

"He's our best chance." Gage couldn't honestly think of another way out. "If he can get us far enough out of town and away from Reyes and his accomplice, then we should be able to take a rideshare the rest of the way."

She nodded and picked up her fork when their dessert arrived. "But detectives don't use police cars, right? I mean, maybe Reyes knows what kind of car he drives."

"I hope to convince the detective to use a squad long enough to take us out of here."

Her expression was skeptical, and he understood it wouldn't be easy. But he was tired of running from bad guys. Especially since every cop in the city should be looking for Reyes.

The pie was good. Not as great as apple, but still good. And he would readily give up apple pie for the rest of his life if that made Darby happy.

"Ready to walk back to the police station?" Darby asked.

"Yeah." He waved down their server and went through what remained of his cash. At some point, he'd need to find an ATM to obtain more.

"I can pay for this one," Darby said.

Since he barely had enough to cover the cost, he slowly nodded. "Once we're safe, I can replenish my cash reserves."

"Me too," Darby agreed.

He grabbed their bags and led the way through the restaurant. He intended to go out first, just in case Reyes or skinny guy was out there with a gun.

Being surrounded by cops offered some protection, but Reyes and his buddy could shoot from a distance, getting away before the cops in the restaurant had time to react.

He hadn't looked over his shoulder this much since he was in prison. And this was worse because he needed to protect Darby.

The walk back to the police precinct didn't take long. The woman behind the desk scowled when they entered. "Now what?"

"Detective Pride asked us to meet him here," Gage explained.

"Hrmph." Her expression was one of annoyance, but she didn't say anything more.

The detective arrived five minutes later. He came in from the back, which was reassuring. "Killion? This way, please."

Gage gestured for Darby to follow the detective. Instead of going into one of the interrogation rooms, Pride led them through an area that was chock-full of desks and cubicles. Some of which had officers sitting at them, but many of which were empty.

"This way." Detective Pride gestured for them to keep following him through another door. Over Darby's shoulder, he could see they were approaching the rear entrance to the police station.

"Detective?"

Pride glanced over his shoulder. "What?"

"Any chance we can take a squad out of here? To avoid being followed?"

To his surprise, the detective smiled. "Yeah, I have a buddy of mine ready to take you guys wherever you need to go."

Gage's gut clenched. "Oh? Who's that?"

"Officer Larry Beacon." Pride narrowed his gaze. "Did you think I'd stick you with Crow?"

"To be honest, I was hoping you would take us yourself," Gage admitted. "We trust you."

A flash of appreciation crossed his features. "Larry is

my brother-in-law, and we went through the academy together. You can trust him too."

Gage nodded. "Okay, thanks."

Minutes later, he and Darby were in the back of a squad that was parked right next to the rear door, with a large transport vehicle blocking any view across the parking lot. He and Darby crouched down very low in the back seat as Detective Pride gave Officer Beacon instructions. "Make sure you aren't followed and keep your eyes open for anyone who looks like Tyrone Reyes."

"Will do," Beacon agreed.

"Can you take us someplace we can get a rideshare?" Gage asked. "Like the nature preserve?"

"I can, yes." Beacon met his gaze in the rearview mirror. "But the country club would be a better spot to pick up a rideshare."

"Yeah, okay." Gage realized he was probably right. "Thanks."

"No problem."

As per Detective Pride's directive, the cop took a roundabout way out of the area. Taking several turns and doubling back more than once. By the time Officer Beacon pulled up near the country club, Gage felt certain that they'd gotten away without being followed by Reyes or skinny guy.

"You both stay safe now, you hear?" Officer Beacon said as he let them out of the back seat.

"We will, thanks." Gage shouldered the bags and took Darby's hand.

"You want me to hang out until the rideshare shows up?"

"Sure." Gage used his phone to call a driver. "Looks like he's less than five minutes away."

"Good." Officer Beacon eyed them for a long moment. "We'll do our best to find this Reyes character."

"Thanks." Gage nodded, appreciating the cop believed them about being in danger. Far different from Officer Crow's attitude.

The rideshare pulled up, the driver asked for Gage. He gave the cop a nod, then opened the door for Darby.

"Can you please take us to Asbury?" Darby asked.

"Yep. Any place in particular?" The driver pulled away from the country club.

Darby thought for a moment. "There's a restaurant called Karen's Kitchen. Could you take us there?"

"Sure." The driver plugged the address into his built-in GPS.

Gage didn't think they'd been followed, but he couldn't help looking frequently out through the back window to scan the traffic behind them. No sign of the black Ford pickup truck.

No sign of anyone else following either.

Darby pulled out her phone. "I'm going to call Edith, let her know we're on our way."

He nodded and listened to her side of the conversation. Darby's voice choked up when she spoke to Leo.

"I love you, Leo. Mommy will be there soon." She sniffled and brushed tears from her eyes. "Be good for Oma."

Darby put her phone away and sat back against the seat cushion. "I can't believe we're finally safe."

"I know." It had been a long haul getting here, but he was glad they'd made it out of East Knoxville without a problem.

"Gage, what if we can't go back?"

Darby's question caught him off guard. "What do you mean?"

"If they don't catch Reyes, we'll never be safe." She turned in her seat to face him. "Unless we disappear forever."

He looked into her clear gray eyes. "We?"

She flushed and nodded. "You need to be safe too, Gage. And I know you want to spend time with Leo."

It was his turn to choke up. He was grateful she'd included him in her plans. But he really hoped it wouldn't come to that. He still had three months of probation that required him to stay in Knoxville. "Let's take it one day at a time. I'm really hoping the police will find Reyes."

"But if they don't," she persisted, "I'm not going back to East Knoxville. Not if there's even the remote possibility of Leo being in danger."

"I know." He truly understood where she was coming from.

Their driver pulled up at the restaurant. Edith and Leo were standing outside waiting for them. Darby bolted from the car, rushing over to scoop Leo up and into her arms. "Oh, I missed you so much," she said.

Gage added a tip for the driver, then grabbed the bags and crossed over to join her. Edith eyed him warily. He offered a smile. "Hi, I'm Gage Killion."

"Edith Schroeder," she responded. "It's nice to meet you."

Darby finally set Leo back on his feet. "Leo, I'd like you to meet—" she faltered, then said, "your daddy."

Leo stuck his fist in his mouth, clutched his mother's leg, and looked up at Gage through green eyes.

His green eyes.

And in that moment, Gage knew he'd go wherever Darby wanted, even if that meant breaking his probation, as long as they could all be together.

CHAPTER THIRTEEN

Darby heard Edith's soft gasp at the news that Gage was Leo's father. Still, she kept her gaze on Gage, who looked at their son with a mixture of hope and love in his eyes. The emotion shimmering from his gaze squeezed her heart.

She was surprisingly glad Gage knew about their son.

Leo was acting unusually shy, so she put a hand on his blond hair and tried to reassure him. "It's okay, Leo. Say hi."

"Hi." Leo's voice was so soft she wasn't sure Gage could hear him.

She gave Gage credit for dropping down into a crouch so he looked less intimidating. "Hi, Leo. I'm really happy to meet you."

Leo clutched her leg tighter. She wasn't sure why he was acting so timid and gently eased his grip from her leg. She knelt beside him. "Leo, your daddy was gone for a while, but now he's back. It's okay, he won't hurt you."

Gage's gaze shot to her as if wondering if their son had been exposed to abuse. She frowned and shook her head. He smiled at Leo. "Have you been swimming?"

Leo finally removed his fist from his mouth. "Yeah, will you swim with me?"

"I'd love to," Gage assured him. Darby's heart melted at the glint of tears in Gage's eyes.

"Maybe after lunch," Edith said. "He spent most of the morning in the pool."

"Can I have chicken fingers?" Leo turned to look up at her hopefully.

"You've had them every day," Edith protested.

Darby glanced at Edith and shrugged. "It won't hurt him. Yes, Leo. You can have chicken fingers for lunch." She kissed the top of his head before rising to her feet. "We'll all sit together."

"Okay." Leo let go of her leg, seeming more like himself. He glanced at Gage. "Do you like chicken fingers?"

"I love them," Gage declared. "Especially with ketchup."

"Me too," Leo said, skipping ahead of them.

Darby suspected Gage would eat mud pies if Leo asked him to and made a mental note to remind Gage that raising a child didn't mean always agreeing with him. Granted, she'd given in on the chicken fingers, but that was a minor concession in the big scheme of things.

And she hadn't wanted to create a fuss while Gage was trying to establish some sort of connection with their son.

Despite the fact that she and Gage had already eaten, the four of them entered the crowded restaurant. They took a seat at a table so she could get a booster seat for Leo. Gage was on one side of Leo while she took the other side. Edith was across from him.

"So, Gage." Edith eyed him over the rim of the plastic menu. "Where do you live?"

"West Knoxville. I work for Morehead Construction. We build houses."

"Oh, that's nice." Edith glanced at Darby. "Is everything taken care of?"

"Not exactly." She wasn't the least bit hungry. "We'll fill you in later, okay?" Darby wasn't going to have this discussion in front of Leo. Not that he'd likely understand it, but she wasn't taking the chance. Leo picked up on things she said far too easily.

"That's fine," Edith agreed.

Their server took the order for Gage's and Leo's chicken fingers and Edith's salad. Darby was happy enough to sip water.

Gage did his best to draw Leo into conversation, asking him about his friends at preschool and what his favorite movie was. Soon Leo was chattering away, all hint of his previous shyness having vanished. She noticed Gage kept his attention centered on the little boy.

It would be good for Leo to have a relationship with his father. And maybe it would be good for her and Gage to work together to raise him. She glanced at Edith, who appeared wary of the situation.

"It's fine, Edith," Darby murmured in a low tone.

"Is it?" Edith leaned closer. "Didn't you tell me Leo's father was in jail?"

"Yes, but Gage has been out for two years now and is doing great."

"How do you know that won't change?" Edith asked.

"I don't," she agreed. "Any more than I know I'll never relapse. I certainly don't plan on going back to my old ways, but none of us can predict the future, can we?"

Only God knows that.

The words popped into her mind as if someone whispered them into her ear. She almost glanced over her shoulder to see if someone was back there.

Only God knows the future. It was something Gage believed with his whole heart.

And maybe he was right. Maybe God did have a master plan for them. Looking at her small family seated around the table, she couldn't help but smile.

Never had she allowed herself to consider being reunited with Gage. If she were honest, she'd admit to staying away from men and relationships in part because of her feelings for him. Despite the fact that things hadn't been very good back then, Gage had remained the bright spot in her life, especially after she'd gotten the courage to dump Aaron.

There was also the fact that she didn't have a lot of spare time to date. And the most important factor that had kept her from seeing anyone was her need to stay sober.

She hadn't wanted to risk trading drugs for alcohol. And most guys didn't understand her desire to drink water or fruit juice.

Frankly, it hadn't been worth the hassle.

That was something she didn't have to worry about with Gage.

When they finished eating, Gage looked upset at not being able to pay. "There must be a cash machine nearby, right?"

"It's my turn," she reminded him. "And yes, we'll both need more cash."

"We should head back to the hotel." Edith glanced at Gage. "Unfortunately, I have a single room with two beds, not a full suite."

"We can upgrade to a two-bedroom suite if one is available," Gage offered. "Or I can sleep on the floor."

Edith nodded and led the way outside. Darby took Leo's hand and was surprised when Gage took the boy's other hand.

"Wheee," he cried, lifting up his feet and putting all his weight on their hands.

Gage chuckled and lifted Leo higher. Darby knew they looked like a happy family as they left the restaurant and headed over to the hotel.

There was a cash machine in the lobby, so she and Gage headed over to replenish their cash reserves. Returning to the front desk, the clerk quickly upgraded them to a two-bedroom suite.

"I wanna swim!" Leo demanded.

Gage glanced over toward the gift shop. "I'll need to get swimming trunks."

"Go ahead, we'll meet you up in the room." Darby handed him one of the keys. "I'll help Edith pack her and Leo's things."

"Thanks." Gage disappeared inside the gift shop.

As they took the elevator to the fourth floor, Leo looked up at her. "Is Daddy going to live with us from now on?"

"Uh, well, I—don't know about that." Darby shot a helpless glance at Edith who shrugged. "He has his apartment, and we have our townhouse. I'm sure you'll get to see him on weekends."

Leo's brow furrowed. "But other mommies and daddies live together."

She blew out a breath, realizing she should have been prepared for this line of questioning. "Some do, but not all."

Leo seemed to consider this response. "Jack's daddy doesn't live with him."

"Exactly." Darby was anxious to change the subject. "Which water ride is your favorite so far?"

"I like the giant slide," Leo declared.

"Sounds fun."

Fifteen minutes later, they were all in the new suite located on the second floor. Once Gage and Leo were ready to swim, they trooped over to the water park.

When father and son went over to try the giant slide, Edith put a hand on her arm. "Gage seems like a nice young man."

"He is." Darby smiled. "We're both in a better place now than we were back then."

"He seems determined to be a role model for Leo." Edith lifted a brow. "Have you discussed child support and visitation arrangements?"

Darby flushed. "We haven't gotten that far. And won't be able to even talk about it until the men who tried to hurt us are arrested."

Edith's expression turned serious. "How long will that take?"

Darby sighed and shook her head. "I don't know. Hopefully soon."

"We can't stay here forever," Edith protested. "What about your job? And Gage's?"

Being gainfully employed was important, but Leo's safety trumped all. "I know we can't stay much longer. I'm hopeful this will all be over very soon."

Darby watched as Gage scooped Leo up into his arms. The little boy was giggling madly as Gage spun in a circle.

She smiled at how father and son looked together.

And silently prayed that God would help the police find Reyes very soon.

GAGE COULDN'T BELIEVE how blessed he was to have this time with Leo. The little boy's initial shyness had finally melted away, revealing a gregarious child who thrived under male attention.

Darby had raised Leo very well. He was kind, polite, yet displayed a hint of stubbornness Gage knew came from his mother.

When he noticed Leo shivering, he picked the boy up and carried him out of the pool.

"No, don't wanna get out," Leo wailed.

He steeled his heart against the plea. "You're shivering, and I'm tired. Look, your mom has towels for us."

"B-but I wanna s-swim." Leo's teeth began to chatter.

"Enough," Darby said firmly. She tossed Gage one of the towels and wrapped the other around their son. "I think it's time to watch a movie."

"A movie?" Just that quickly Leo gave up on swimming. "Which one?"

"Hmm." Darby pretended to consider this. "*Cars*?"

"*Cars*!" Leo shouted with glee. "I love *Cars*!"

Gage hated to admit he'd never seen it. Movies weren't high on his list of things to do. Work, sleep, eat, and attend church services, plus the Saturday night basketball games were the sum total of his life.

Some of which would need to change now that he had Leo to consider.

They returned to the suite. By the time he'd showered off the chlorine and changed, he found Leo already dressed and snuggled in front of the television where cartoon cars were talking to each other.

"He'll probably fall asleep," Edith confided. "He never wants to take a nap, but he'll end up sleeping anyway."

Gage nodded. He'd spent plenty of time in the water

with Leo but found he wanted, needed more. He wished he could hold the boy in his lap and simply watch him while he slept.

His phone rang before he could act on his thoughts. Recognizing Detective Pride's number, he quickly answered, moving away for privacy. "Hi, Detective. I hope you're calling with good news."

"Not exactly," Pride admitted. "I wanted to let you know we found the black Ford truck with the stolen plate. It was abandoned in the parking lot of a grocery store."

A wave of frustration threatened to crush him. "I don't understand. How is it possible you haven't found Reyes yet?"

"You said the driver of the truck was a skinny guy, someone other than Reyes," Pride pointed out.

"That's correct. But still, that BOLO has been out on Reyes for two days now. He can't be that hard to find."

"We don't know for sure he's stayed in the area," Pride countered. "Could be he hightailed it out of town and left skinny guy to clean up after him."

That possibility hadn't occurred to him. He wished he'd gotten a better look at the driver of the truck. "What are we supposed to do? Our lives have already been put on hold, and Darby and I both need to get back to work."

"I know, I'm sorry to be the bearer of bad news."

Gage bit back his annoyance. This wasn't Detective Pride's fault.

He was the one who'd worked for Reyes. Who'd turned Reyes and Archer in to the authorities. Now Archer was dead and Reyes was in the wind.

He had no clue who skinny guy was. Could be someone Gage once worked with, or he could be a total stranger, someone he'd never seen before.

"Gage? You still there?" Detective Pride asked.

"Yes. I'm here." Gage looked over to where Leo leaned against his mother, his eyelids already growing heavy. "Any word on what may have caused Niles Archer's death? Did the ME rule it a suicide?"

Pride paused for a moment before responding. "Archer's death was deemed inconclusive."

Gage frowned. "What does that mean?"

"It means the ME couldn't rule out murder or suicide."

Gage let that information sink in for a moment. "So, Reyes may have paid someone to murder him."

"We have no proof of that," Pride said.

"You have some proof he didn't die by his own hand," Gage countered.

Pride sighed heavily. "Leave the investigating to us. Just stay safe, okay?"

"We'll try." He felt guilty for the hint of sarcasm and added, "We appreciate the update, Detective."

"You're welcome." Pride disconnected from the call.

He slid his phone into his pocket. Darby eased from a now sleeping Leo and came over to him. "You look upset. What's wrong?" she whispered.

Gage quickly filled her in.

"Inconclusive," she repeated. "Maybe Officer Crow is involved?"

"The sheriff's department runs the jail, but it's certainly possible Crow has buddies who work there."

Darby glanced over to where Edith was sitting and reading. "Let's take a walk."

Gage nodded. "Are you sure Edith won't mind?"

"She can relax while Leo naps. I'll tell her to call me when he wakes up." Darby crossed over and spoke to Edith who smiled and nodded.

Gage had the impression that Edith liked giving them time together. As if Leo's Oma was hoping for a rekindling of their former relationship.

He couldn't lie, he wanted the very same thing. Yet being in danger and hiding out from Reyes wasn't exactly a good time to discuss that.

They left the hotel room and headed outside. The hotel was busy for a weekday, and with the weekend coming up, he could only imagine the activity would grow exponentially.

His life was solitary and quiet. Playing with Leo in the water had been fun, but the idea of spending endless days here didn't appeal to him.

"I feel safe here," Darby said as they walked down to the road.

"Me too." He glanced at her. "How much longer do you think we should stay?"

She lifted a brow. "How did you know I was going to talk to you about that?"

"It's been on my mind too." Gage took her hand in his. "This is fun for Leo, but it's also not realistic to stay indefinitely. The rooms here are pricey."

"Tell me about it," Darby muttered. "I'm using up most of my savings to fund this."

"Maybe it's time to consider relocating somewhere new." Gage hadn't been ready to do something that drastic when Darby mentioned it earlier, but getting the update from Pride had convinced him there was no end in sight.

The longer Reyes went without getting caught, the more likely the guy had skipped town for a while. And if that was the case, Gage wasn't going to risk Reyes coming back to find them again a few weeks from now.

"Will you get in trouble if we leave Knoxville?"

He glanced at her. "I could, yes. I'm technically due to come off parole in less than three months. But I'm probably not high risk enough for the police to track me down to arrest me." At least, he hoped not. "If we stay in touch with Detective Pride, I'm sure he can hold the arrest warrant at bay."

"You think he'll do that?" Darby's eyes filled with hope.

"I hope so." Pride was a decent guy and understood the magnitude of the danger they faced. He wouldn't necessarily like it, but Gage felt certain the detective would go along with his plan. "My bigger concern is our ability to find jobs."

Some of the light in Darby's eyes faded. "Yeah, I know. That won't be easy with our past."

"Especially my criminal record." Gage sighed. "I can ask my old boss for a reference, even though he won't be happy to lose me without warning."

"Kent will be the same way," Darby admitted.

Gage straightened his shoulders in an attempt to remain strong. "I won't go back to selling drugs."

"I won't go back to using either," Darby said. "Leo deserves better." She hesitated, then added, "We'll figure something out."

"Okay." He turned so they could head back to the hotel. "So we leave tomorrow?"

She nodded. "May as well. We paid for tonight, so one more day won't matter."

"And what will Edith say?"

Darby grimaced. "She won't be happy about it. But I think she'll go along in order to keep Leo safe."

He nodded, hoping she was right. No matter where they ended up, they'd need Edith's help with Leo, especially as they looked for work. "Did she say anything about me?"

"Who, Edith?"

"Yeah. I know she was surprised that I popped back into your life."

"She was wary at first, but she thinks you're a nice guy." Darby slanted him a glance. "I reassured her that you were."

"Thanks." That was one less issue to worry about. "Thank you for raising Leo. You did an amazing job with him."

Darby looked pleased by the comment. "Honestly, Edith gets a lot of credit. I never knew my mother, so I was constantly worried about whether or not I was doing right by Leo."

"You're a wonderful mother."

She rolled her eyes. "Says you after a few hours. Trust me, there are times I'm ready to yank my hair out. Leo is a great kid, but he can be stubborn too."

"I noticed. He gets that from you."

She swatted at him. "No, he gets that from you."

He stopped and pulled her into his arms. "Darby, he's the best of both of us."

Her eyes softened. "He is."

Gage kissed her, and the flare of passion they'd once shared sprang between them. He kissed her for a full minute before reluctantly letting her go.

"Wow," she murmured.

"Yeah, wow." He took her hand and forced himself to go back inside the hotel. "I still care about you, Darby."

"I—care about you too." There was a slight hesitation in her tone.

"But?"

She sighed. "I don't want to rush into anything. And I

don't want to confuse Leo. He's only just learned you exist, I don't think we should do anything we might later regret."

Her comment stung. "I'm not going to regret caring about you."

"Not just that, but Leo already asked if we were going to live together." Darby glanced at him as they walked through the lobby. "I don't want us to be together, then separate, then get back together again."

She was describing their old life, one he had no interest in returning to. "I understand, but we're different people now."

"Yes, but we've also just reunited after six years apart." She jabbed the button for the elevator. "I don't want to repeat the mistakes of the past, Gage. I plan to keep taking things one day at a time."

"Yeah, okay." He could somewhat understand her position, yet he also sensed she was holding back. Maybe afraid of getting too close.

He told himself to be patient, but he knew it wouldn't be easy. Huh. Maybe Leo had inherited some stubbornness from him after all.

They walked down the hallway to their suite. Darby used her key to enter and stopped so abruptly in her tracks that her head reared back to hit his chin.

"Well, it's about time you two showed up." Tyrone Reyes stood there holding a gun on Edith and Leo. "I've been waiting."

Ice coalesced in his veins as he understood that Reyes hadn't left town after all.

The man he'd once betrayed intended to kill them all.

CHAPTER FOURTEEN

Darby barely registered Gage bumping into her as she stared in horror at Reyes. The drug dealer was approximately six feet away from Edith and Leo, and she knew with terrible certainty he wouldn't miss if he decided to shoot them.

No, please, God, not Leo. Please don't let him shoot my son!

It was difficult to ignore Leo's crying as he clung to his oma, but she kept her gaze pinned to Reyes. She took some hope in the fact that he hadn't immediately started shooting.

"It's me you want, Tyrone," she said in an oddly calm voice. She took another step into the room. "I'll go with you without a problem. There's no reason to hurt the woman and the boy."

"Close the door, Killion," Reyes snapped.

The sound of the hotel room door clicking shut could be heard above Leo's sobs. Darby didn't bother to glance back at Gage, her entire being was focused on Reyes. She took another step forward, desperate to get through to him. "I'll go with you, Tyrone, and so will Gage. You don't want to shoot that gun here, too many people are around to hear the sound and call the police."

"You both deserve to die." Reyes spat the words, anger darkening his eyes. "And I'm here to make sure that happens."

Darby wasn't worried about her own life. She didn't have a death wish or anything, but she would not hesitate to sacrifice herself for her son. "I know you will," she admitted. "But the question is whether or not you want to get away with it. Again, shooting us here is only going to bring everyone running. This isn't the Knotty Pine, it's a family hotel. The cops will descend on this place before you can blink." She gave an exaggerated shrug. "Why take the risk when you can easily take us somewhere else?"

"Put your hands where I can see them," Reyes barked.

Her hands were at her sides in clear view, so she knew he was addressing Gage. "I'm not armed, and neither is Gage." She eased forward another step in an attempt to get close enough that she could throw herself at Reyes. It was the only thing she could think of to do, and she trusted that Gage would react quickly enough to save their son.

Edith would do her part too.

Darby couldn't imagine life without Leo, so she didn't dwell on the possibility of Reyes killing her. Nothing mattered as long as Leo was safe.

"As Darby said, I'm not armed," Gage said from behind her. "But you should listen to her logic, Reyes. Shooting us here in a hotel isn't very smart. Better to be outside where it will be easier for you to escape."

"Mommy!" Leo's cries grew louder, wrenching her heart. Still, she didn't dare take her eyes off Reyes. If he so much as pointed the gun at her baby . . .

"Shut him up!" Reyes shouted, startling her.

"Yelling isn't going to help," Darby said. "You're scaring him. I already told you, we'll go with you."

"The kid's crying could cause someone to call and complain," Gage added. "Hotel security could show up at any moment."

"Leave the woman and the child alone," Darby said firmly. "They are not a threat to you. But if you kill them, the police will not rest until they find you."

For a moment, Reyes looked uncertain as to what he should do. Darby wanted to believe that deep down Tyrone didn't want to kill a child. But she also knew she may be giving him more credit than he deserved.

"No one is going anywhere," Reyes barked.

Darby slid one more step closer. She tried to estimate how long they'd been caught and held in this terrifying standoff. It felt like forever but was likely barely two minutes.

Two minutes and Reyes was already losing his cool. Darby knew she couldn't linger much longer. She'd need to act before Reyes began shooting.

Gage lightly tugged on the back of her shirt as if silently warning her not to do anything. How he'd known what she'd planned, she had no idea. Not that it mattered. She wasn't going to let him hold her back while Reyes threatened their son.

She had to trust that Gage would do his part. "Okay, Tyrone," she said quietly. "We won't go anywhere. But I think you need to reconsider your plan, as it has a few holes in it."

Leo abruptly screamed, "Mommy!"

The unexpected sound diverted Reyes's attention just enough, and Darby reacted instinctively. She leaped forward and shoved as hard as she could against Reyes's gun hand in an effort to knock the weapon loose.

A loud retort echoed as the gun went off. Darby's ears rang, but she thought she heard the weapon hit the floor.

"No!" Reyes shouted.

Gage had followed her lead and had jumped on Reyes, knocking him backward. Darby spun to face the two men wrestling for the upper hand. Gage was younger and stronger, but that didn't mean Reyes was a pushover. Glancing frantically around the room, she spied a lamp. Rushing forward, she picked it up and held it, waiting for the opportunity to strike.

Reyes had his hands wrapped around Gage's neck. Bitter fear coated her tongue as she noticed that Gage appeared to be weakening. With a surge of strength, Reyes rolled over so he was on top of Gage.

Darby brought the lamp crashing down on Reyes's head. The ceramic base shattered at the impact. Reyes went limp, and Gage quickly escaped.

"Mommy! Mommy!" Leo continued to scream and cry out for her.

She turned to see Edith curling her body around the little boy. Darby dropped to her knees beside them. "Are you okay? Are you hurt?" She frantically searched for any sign of blood.

"Fine," Edith managed in a squeaky voice. "We're fine. The bullet hit the wall."

Darby moved her gaze to the side, noting the small round hole in the drywall. So close.

Too close.

She gathered Leo close, soothing him. Moments later, there was a loud pounding on the hotel room door.

"Gage? Darby? It's Detective Pride! Open up!"

The detective? She frowned and looked over at Gage who was using the cord from the broken lamp to bind Reyes's hands together.

"I called him on my phone," Gage said. His face was ashen as he rose. "But this seems like too quick of a response."

Remembering how they'd suspected Crow of being involved spurred her into action. She thrust Leo back into Edith's arms. "Take him and hide in the bathroom," she whispered. "Don't come out until we tell you it's safe."

Edith gave a terse nod. Darby helped the older woman stand. Edith hurried out of the living area of the suite as Gage went over to look through the peephole.

"What do you see?" Darby whispered.

"Nothing." Gage moved to the side of the door. "Whoever is out there is standing out of view."

"Open up! Police!"

A wave of uncertainty washed over her. She didn't know who they could trust. Was Detective Pride really out there? Or was it Officer Crow?

Gage pulled out his phone, pressed a button, and held the device to his ear. "Pride? Where are you?"

"Outside your hotel room," Pride answered. "Let us in."

She relaxed, but Gage kept talking. "How did you get here from Knoxville so fast?"

"I wasn't in Knoxville, I was on my way here," Pride admitted. "Seriously, Gage, open the door."

Gage looked at her. "What do you think?"

She shrugged. "I don't think we can hide out in here forever."

"Hand me Reyes's gun," Gage said.

She glanced over to where the weapon was lying on the floor. Crossing over, she gingerly picked it up. "You can't have this in your hand when they come in," she whispered. "It's a parole violation."

"I don't care, I'm not letting them in without being armed," Gage said tersely.

"I'll keep it." She stood near Reyes who was still unconscious from being hit by the lamp. "Let them in."

"Give it to me," Gage insisted.

"Killion!" More pounding on the door. "Open up!"

She stood with the dreaded gun and nodded at Gage. "Open it."

Looking frustrated, Gage finally opened the door just a crack. Instantly, someone kicked it open, knocking him off balance.

Darby swung the gun toward the door but relaxed when she saw Detective Pride and two other police officers.

Not Crow.

"Put down the gun," one of the officers yelled.

Darby pointed the barrel toward the ceiling. "Okay, I'm putting it down. Oh, and the gun belongs to Tyrone Reyes. He threatened to kill us all, including my five-year-old son."

Pride looked down at the bits of ceramic lamp scattered across the floor and the cord wrapped around Reyes's wrists. "Good job," he said.

Darby lowered herself to the floor to set the gun down. Then she stumbled toward Gage, throwing herself into his arms.

It was over.

GAGE CRADLED Darby close while keeping a wary eye on Detective Pride. He had called the guy while Darby was holding Reyes's attention, but he still didn't understand how on earth the cop had gotten to Asbury so quickly. Pride claimed to have been on his way, but that didn't make sense either.

"How did you know we were here?" Gage asked.

Pride turned to face him. "You're insinuating I'm a part of this?" His tone was incredulous. "You called me, remember? I heard Darby talking to Reyes."

"I don't know what to think," Gage admitted. "You said you were on your way, but I didn't tell you where we were going."

Pride sighed. "I'm a cop, Killion. I've been watching your bank cards and saw that you used them to secure this room."

That news wasn't exactly reassuring. "Why would you do that? We're the victims, not the suspects."

Pride lifted a hand. "I didn't say you were suspects, but I also needed to keep an eye on you." He glanced back down to Reyes who let out a low groan. "Good thing I was heading over here to let you know what I found out."

Darby pulled from his embrace. He forced himself to let her go. "I need to get Edith and Leo, they've been scared to death."

Pride watched as Darby disappeared into one of the bedrooms. Then he swung back to face Gage. "Wow, you really didn't trust me, did you?"

"No." Gage let out a breath. "But you can't blame me. It seems like Reyes has been on our tail the entire time."

Pride gestured to one of the cops. "Cuff him properly and call an ambulance. He needs medical attention."

Gage stepped back to give the officers room to maneuver. They removed the lamp cord he'd used and replaced it with silver cuffs. Reyes groaned again as they hauled him into a sitting position.

"He hit me," Reyes accused in a weak voice. "That's assault and battery."

"Read him his rights," Pride suggested. "Reyes, if you're smart, you'll keep your mouth shut."

Darby returned to the living room carrying Leo. Edith walked beside her, the poor woman looking as if she'd aged ten years after nearly being shot to death. Darby made quick introductions.

"That man pretended to be hotel security." Edith pointed a shaky finger at Reyes. "I should have recognized him from the photo Darby sent me, but I didn't. He forced his way into the room and held us at gunpoint as we waited for Gage and Darby to arrive."

"Ms. Schroeder, I'm very sorry you had to go through that terrible experience." Pride's gaze was full of compassion. "Please have a seat. I'll take your statement in a moment."

"Mine too?" Darby asked. "And Gage's?"

Pride nodded. "But we need to talk to each of you, separately."

Edith frowned and nodded. "Of course."

Gage was relieved to note Leo had stopped crying. But it still pained him at how the little boy clung to Darby as if he might never let her go.

Guilt assailed him. He should have done more to protect them. How had Reyes followed them anyway? Pride had known where they were staying, was it possible Officer Crow had found their location and leaked it to Reyes?

He wanted to talk to Pride first. "Detective? I'd like to give you my statement."

Pride lifted a brow and nodded. "Okay, let's go into the other room."

Gage followed him, pausing just enough to lightly

stroke a hand down Leo's back. He wanted so badly to be the one to comfort the child, but he was still essentially a stranger to his own son.

A situation he needed to rectify and soon.

He sat on the edge of the bed as Pride took the only chair in the room. "Start at the beginning," the detective suggested.

Gage went through the series of events as succinctly as possible. When he described how Darby rushed Reyes, Pride's eyes widened in surprise.

"That was a huge risk," Pride said.

"I wasn't happy either, but he'd threatened her son." Gage shook his head. "If I'd have gone into the room first, and been in the right position, I'd have done the same thing."

"Go on," Pride urged.

The rest of the story didn't take long. Obviously the detective had seen the broken lamp and the cord he'd used to tie up Reyes. To his credit, Pride appeared to believe his story and didn't make Gage go back over every detail several times.

"Okay, I'm sure Darby's story will match, but I still need to hear it for myself," Pride said. "Will you send her in?"

Gage didn't move. "Before I get Darby, I need to know how Reyes found us."

Pride's eyes narrowed. "How would I know?"

"You arranged for the cop to drop us off at the country club, and we took a rideshare from there to a restaurant, before coming to the hotel." Gage held the detective's gaze. "I don't see how Reyes would have gotten here so fast without help."

A flash of anger darkened Pride's eyes. "You're back to

accusing a cop of leaking information?"

Gage spread his hands. "You tell me."

Pride glared at him. "Well, now I see why you didn't trust me at the door."

"Exactly." Gage wasn't going to apologize for his suspicions. "You had inside information from our bank information. Reyes shouldn't have access to that. But if he did, he got it from someone."

Pride ground his teeth together. "Okay, I see what you're saying. I've been keeping an eye on Crow, but a cop at his level wouldn't have access to your bank information."

"But he could have seen it or heard you talk about it at some point," Gage argued. "I saw him at the 799 restaurant. He smirked at me from across the room."

"I can't accuse a cop of being dirty because he smirked," Pride snapped.

"No, but you can tell IAB that his actions need to be investigated." Gage kept his tone even. "In fact, that's the least you can do after this fiasco."

"I'm not the one who double-crossed Reyes," Pride shot back.

"No, I did that," Gage acknowledged. He leaned forward. "But you and the entire Knoxville police department were looking for him. Haven't you asked yourself how he managed to elude you for so long? He almost killed us all." The close call still sent shivers down his spine. "The guy isn't that good. He should have been spotted before now."

There was a long tense moment as the detective stared at him. "Yeah, okay. You have a point. We should have gotten Reyes in custody before he could threaten you and Darby at gunpoint. But that isn't proof Officer Crow is involved."

"If not Crow, then someone else." Gage wasn't giving up his theory. "I'd feel much better if you'd at least talk to the guy."

Pride looked down at his notebook for a moment. "Anything else?" he finally asked.

"Yeah, why were you coming here anyway?"

Pride nodded. "Oh, yeah, I forgot to tell you about that. We found DNA under Steve Auckland's fingernails. I wanted to get a sample from you and Darby to exclude you."

"Exclude us?" Gage battled a wave of outrage. "We're the victims here."

"I know, but you both have criminal records." Detective Pride didn't back down from his outburst. "And the best way to move forward with the investigation is to clear you both as suspects."

Gage stood and dragged a hand over his hair. He took several deep breaths to get his anger and frustration under control. In hindsight, he should be glad Detective Pride had been on his way to Asbury to get their DNA. He had no doubt that if just the local authorities had answered the call, he and Darby would both be in jail.

"Okay, yeah, you can take my DNA." Gage finally turned to look at the Detective. "I can't speak for Darby."

Pride slowly rose. "It would help for you to let her know you're willing to cooperate."

"Sure." He was hit by a wave of exhaustion. Not so much because of the physical bruises he sustained while fighting with Reyes.

Emotionally. It seemed like he and Darby had been hiding for so long, facing danger at every turn.

He wanted to believe that with Reyes in custody, their nightmare was over.

"What about the stolen black truck?"

Pride frowned as his abrupt question. "What about it?"

"Did you find any fingerprints?" Gage stared at the detective. "I know for sure the driver of that truck wasn't Reyes."

"The truck is being processed by the crime scene techs," Pride said. "I haven't heard anything about them lifting any prints."

Gage knew it was possible skinny guy had worn gloves, but June in Knoxville was hot, even with the shade of the mountains. A guy wearing gloves would be noticed. "Reyes must know who skinny guy is," he muttered.

"And we'll ask him," Pride assured him. "But that will take some time considering he needs medical care thanks to getting bashed on the head."

"I'm not going to apologize for that."

"I didn't ask you to," Pride said. "But that doesn't change the fact that I can't question Reyes until he's medically cleared. And I'm sure he'll ask for a lawyer regardless. He's well versed on the legal system."

Gage hated to admit he was right. No way would they learn anything about Reyes's accomplice anytime soon. Feeling dejected, Gage nodded and moved to the door. "I'll get Darby."

"Gage?"

He turned to face Pride. "Yeah?"

"Good work in taking Reyes down." The detective offered a wry smile. "I'm sorry you had to go through that, but the good news is that we got him. And his having a gun is a parole violation. He'll be back in jail the minute he's medically stable."

"Yeah, that's good. But it would be better if you could keep him behind bars for the rest of his life."

"If we can tie him to Auckland's murder, he'll get life without parole."

Gage tried to stay positive. He crossed through the door and found Darby and Leo sitting on the sofa. The little boy had finally loosened his grip on his mother and was playing with a toy car. One that was identical to the car featured in the cartoon. "Darby, Detective Pride is ready to talk to you."

"Okay." She searched his gaze. "How did it go?"

"Fine." He glanced over to where the cop was watching them. "Nothing to worry about."

"Leo, will you wait here for me?" Darby addressed the boy. "You can sit here by your daddy."

The little boy eyed him curiously. Gage sank down beside his son. "Will you show me your car?"

"Vroom," Leo said, swiping the car across the sofa cushion.

"Very cool," Gage said, engaging with the boy so Darby could ease away.

"Do you have a car?" Leo asked.

"I have a truck." Gage smiled. "Do you know what a truck looks like?"

Leo nodded and ran his car along the side of Gage's jean-clad leg. "I like trucks."

"Me too." Gage absently played with his son, his mind whirling. Since skinny guy was still out there, somewhere, he didn't dare allow Darby, Leo, and Edith to head back to their townhouse.

At least, not yet.

Unfortunately, they'd have to remain hidden a while longer. And this time, he'd make sure they were unable to be tracked electronically by using their bank cards.

Pride might trust Crow, but Gage didn't. Not with Darby's and Leo's lives at stake.

CHAPTER FIFTEEN

Darby went through the sequence of events with Detective Pride, ending with the moment she brought the lamp down on Reyes's head.

"You took a risk going for his gun like that." Pride frowned. "You're lucky you weren't shot."

"Better me than Leo." She regarded the detective steadily. "Under the exact same circumstances, I'd do it all again."

He sighed. "And the next time, you could easily be seriously injured or worse."

She thought about how Gage had insisted that God was watching over them and couldn't deny she'd prayed more in the past two days than she had in her entire life. Scarred by the Preacher, she realized now that Gage was right to stay focused on the positive side of things.

God may have helped all the foster kids escape the fire that fateful night. And God may have been guiding her when she went through rehab, gave birth to Leo, and met Edith.

"Darby?"

Pride's voice broke into her thoughts. "Uh, sorry, I missed your question."

"Can you remember exactly what Reyes said to you?"

She thought back. "He honestly didn't say much. He told us he was waiting for us and to get inside the room. He told Gage to get his hands up where he could see them." She slowly shook her head. "I was so focused on inching closer to him so I could try to get the gun away from Leo that I can't remember anything else."

"You have no idea how he found you here at the hotel?"

She shrugged. "I assume he must have managed to follow us. Although how he managed that with the precautions we took is difficult to comprehend." Then she remembered Gage's suspicions about Officer Crow. "Reyes could have gotten inside information from someone."

"Someone?"

She flushed under his flash of anger. "You have to admit it's possible."

"There are plenty of ways Reyes could have found you," Pride said tersely.

"You need to do your part in keeping us safe," she shot back. "A five-year-old shouldn't be held at gunpoint."

A pained expression crossed his features. "I know. And I am working on that." Pride glanced down at his notebook. "Do you have anything else to add?"

"No." She rose. "I would appreciate it if you'd refrain from questioning Leo. I think he's been frightened enough as it is."

"I won't. But I'd like to speak with Edith, to understand how Reyes got inside the room."

She wanted to reiterate what Edith had told her, but she knew the detective would prefer to hear the information firsthand. Upon returning to the living area, she crossed over to Edith. "You're next."

The woman who'd been like a mother to her stood. "When he's finished questioning us, we can leave?"

"Yes." She gave Edith a quick hug. "I'm sorry you had to go through this."

"I'm just glad it's over." Edith hugged her back, then crossed over to the bedroom to speak with the detective.

Darby's gaze landed on Leo and Gage. They were playing with a couple of cars, and just seeing them together made her smile.

Gage would be a part of Leo's life from now on. Gage was already acting like a father, and Leo certainly deserved to have Gage nearby.

They'd have to figure out a way to make it work. She was relieved Reyes had been arrested, but the fact that they'd been found here in Asbury still worried her.

Gage glanced at her, and she could see the same concern darkening his gaze. "When Edith is finished, we'll need to pack our things."

"I know." She honestly didn't want to stay here anyway. The memory of Reyes holding a gun pointed at her son was too fresh in her mind. "Do you have a plan?"

Gage nodded. "Sort of. But I'll fill you in later."

One of the local cops still stood in the doorway, and she realized Gage didn't feel comfortable speaking freely in front of him. By the scowl on the officer's face, he wasn't too happy about that either.

In the past, she and Gage had spent a lot of time hiding from the police, working hard not to get caught with the goods. Gage had been far better at eluding the authorities. Her drug use had skewed her ability to think clearly, which is how she'd gotten caught. In her defense, she'd just learned she was pregnant and had left their apartment in a rush because she'd been too afraid to tell Gage. When the cop had confronted her, she'd been too stunned to react quickly enough to escape.

And then she'd gone a step further, betraying Gage in order to go into rehab rather than jail. A decision that she'd agonized over at the time. It hadn't seemed fair to turn Gage in to the police as he'd always been nice to her.

Unlike Aaron Dukes. In hindsight, she should have added Aaron to the list she'd given the police that night. At the time, she hadn't seen Aaron in several months, but she still could have told them what little she knew about him.

Nothing she could do to fix that now, though. It was still surprising to her that Gage wasn't holding a grudge against her for that.

Because he'd found God.

She looked again at how easily Leo played cars with Gage. Maybe it was time for her to open her heart and her mind to faith and God.

Not just for herself, but for her son.

A few minutes later, Edith and Detective Pride emerged from the room. Darby stepped forward. "Are we free to go?"

Pride nodded. "Where are you headed?"

"Not sure yet." Gage left Leo on the sofa to join her. "All you need to know is that we're going off-grid. I'm not saying anything more. I refuse to take a chance on someone finding us again."

Pride looked as if he wanted to argue, but he didn't. Instead, he reluctantly nodded. "Understood."

"You need to find the skinny guy who stole the black Ford truck," Gage added. "He's still out there, somewhere."

Darby suppressed a slight shiver. Skinny guy was the

only threat that remained, unless of course Reyes had someone within the police department on his payroll.

"I'll check in with the crime scene techs on whether or not they found anything on the truck," Pride agreed.

Darby figured if there were prints in the truck, they'd have found them already. She helped Edith pack their things. It didn't take long, except for gathering Leo's toys, which happened to be strewn all over the suite.

"Okay, Leo, time to go," Darby said.

"Noooo, don't wanna." Leo whined and held a small plastic car firmly in each hand. "Wanna stay."

"We can't stay," Darby said. "We'll find someplace new."

"With a water slide?" Leo asked.

She glanced helplessly at Gage. "I don't think so."

"I wanna swim." Leo's green eyes filled with tears. Darby knew he was overtired and likely still suffering from anxiety after Reyes had threatened him with a gun.

"Not today," Gage said firmly. "Listen to your mother."

Leo eyed him warily, as if unsure whether or not he should comply. But when Leo turned toward her, she stepped up beside Gage, providing a united front. "You heard us, Leo. We're leaving now."

Edith came over and held out her hand. Leo reluctantly took it. Gage shouldered their bags, and they walked through the hotel lobby, past several police cars still parked outside the building.

"Police cars," Leo said with enthusiasm.

"Yes," Darby agreed, glancing at Gage, who swept his gaze over the vehicles as they passed by.

"This way," Edith said. "My car is over in the small parking structure across the street."

"Your car?" Gage glanced at her in surprise.

"How did you think we got here from Knoxville?" Edith asked. "We certainly didn't fly."

"I—guess it never occurred to me." Gage's expression turned thoughtful. "I'm not sure if we should take your car, could be that Reyes stumbled across it, which is how he knew you were here."

"No way could he have known which room we were in," Darby insisted. "Not without inside information."

Gage nodded thoughtfully. "I guess taking the rideshare from the country club didn't help much."

"It should have." Darby paused at the bottom of the hill, feeling the keen gaze from several of the officers standing near their squads. "We could take another rideshare out of here, but we'd need Leo's booster seat from the car."

Gage considered that for a moment before turning to Edith. "How long has the car been in the structure?"

"Since we arrived." Edith waved a hand. "Everything has been within walking distance, so I haven't used the car once."

"Besides, if Reyes had followed Edith's car, he would have showed up well before now," Darby pointed out. "Edith and Leo been here for the past three days."

"Not necessarily. Remember, you and I were his main targets," Gage countered. "We know he orchestrated several attempts against us."

And likely had arranged for Archer's murder.

She glanced at Leo, hoping the little boy wasn't following their conversation too closely. "I still think Reyes would have shown up here sooner if he knew their location. It was the quickest and easiest way to get to us." As he ultimately had. Darby would have easily given her life for her son's.

"We shouldn't stand around talking about it," Edith said

briskly. "I say we get to the car and drive for a while. We can always come up with an alternative plan once we're out of Asbury."

"Sounds good," Gage agreed.

"Yes, but where are we going?" Darby asked.

Gage grimaced. "Not back to Knoxville, that's for sure. I was thinking Seymour. They have a few hotels there."

Darby tried not to wince at the idea of staying at yet another hotel. She understood the need to remain hidden, but for how much longer?

She and Gage didn't have enough money to do this indefinitely.

Not to mention they both had jobs they couldn't afford to lose. She also didn't want Gage to violate his parole. His ending up in prison again wasn't part of the plan.

"This way," Edith said, gesturing for them to follow. From here, Darby could see the modest two-story concrete parking structure. She took Leo's hand as they crossed the street and headed down the road to the right where the entrance of the structure was located. There were many cars parked there, the hotel was obviously experiencing a great surge in summer tourism. Edith led them toward the far left back corner of the first floor of the structure.

Edith's vehicle was a gold Chevy Lumina with less miles than what Darby had on her Accord. Well, her former Accord. It was toast now.

The nice thing about covered parking is that it prevented the sun from heating the interior of the vehicle to unbearable heat levels.

Still, even with being parked under cover, a wave of stale hot air greeted Darby when she opened the passenger side door. "Ugh."

"Open all the doors to air it out," Gage suggested as he

placed their bags in the trunk. When he finished, he approached Edith with his palm up. "Would you mind letting me drive?"

"Of course not." She dropped the keys into his palm.

"Do you know where Seymour is?" Darby asked as she buckled Leo into his booster seat. "If not, I can drive."

She'd no sooner finished with Leo when a man emerged from behind one of the large concrete pillars holding up the second story. The blood drained from her face when she saw the gun in his hand and recognized him as Aaron Dukes.

"Well, well. Looky what I found." Aaron's smile didn't hold any humor. In fact, there was an evil darkness in his eyes that reminded her of the Preacher. She shivered as sweat slipped down her spine.

"Aaron." Darby tried not to show the extent of her fear and revulsion. "Reyes has already been arrested, and I know he won't hesitate to rat you out. If you were smart, you'd get far away from here, especially considering there are several cops hanging around the hotel. Whatever revenge you're seeking isn't worth getting arrested, is it?"

"I don't care about Reyes or the cops. I got friends in high places." Aaron's gaze pierced her. "I want you, Darby. If you want the others to live, you'll come with me."

Her heart thudded painfully against her chest. The last thing she wanted was to go anywhere near Aaron.

But she didn't want him near her son either.

With a sick sense of certainty, Darby knew she had little choice but to comply with Aaron's demand.

GAGE FINALLY UNDERSTOOD that Darby's former boyfriend, Aaron Dukes, was the skinny guy they'd glimpsed driving the black Ford. He eased his hand into his pocket to use his phone. Calling Pride had worked before, he hoped and prayed it would work again now.

Aaron wasn't wearing gloves, which meant his fingerprints would be all over the gun. If they found a way out of this mess.

"Now, Darby," Aaron barked. He lifted the gun up and aimed the muzzle directly at Gage. "Or I start shooting."

"Why?" Gage asked, trying to divert the guy's attention. "What's the point of shooting us all, bringing the cops rushing over to arrest you?"

"The point is, I want Darby," Aaron repeated between clenched teeth. "Get moving or we'll all die here. Including the brat."

Gage winced at the way Darby reacted to his reference to Leo. "Okay, I'll come with you." Darby took a step toward Aaron. "But you need to put the gun away."

No! Gage curled his fingers into fists. He was not going to let Darby go anywhere near that creep. He didn't trust him not to shoot them all anyway.

"Yeah, right," Aaron sneered. "Not happening. Get over here, Darby." Aaron turned so the gun was now pointing at Edith. "Or the old lady goes first."

"I said I'm coming," Darby snapped. "Excuse me for finding it difficult to walk toward a maniac holding a gun."

Gage swallowed hard as the muzzle of the gun swung toward Darby. At that short of a distance, even an idiot like Aaron wouldn't miss.

"Maniac?" Aaron repeated, his voice dangerously soft.

Darby instantly realized her mistake. "I'm sorry. But can't you see you're scaring me?"

"You should be scared," Aaron taunted. "You never should have left me for *him*." Now he jabbed the gun toward Gage.

From the inexpert prison tattoos decorating Aaron's hands and forearms, Gage knew Aaron had been locked up for a significant period of time. If not, he would have come after Darby a long time ago.

And prison was likely how Aaron Dukes had teamed up with Reyes. Both guys must have stayed at a high security prison, whereas he'd been sent to a lower security facility.

A blessing, truly, or these guys would have made his life miserable over those four years. Gage needed God's grace and wisdom to get out of this now.

Come on, Pride, he silently urged. Hurry up and find us.

His position behind the car didn't help the situation. Darby was the closest to Aaron. Edith too. They'd both been along the passenger side of the car.

He had the driver's side door open about an inch. He eased it open a little more, needing enough room to hit the horn. The sound would summon others to the area.

But it could also push Aaron over the edge, causing him to start shooting.

Gage hesitated, torn with indecision.

"Where are you taking me?" Darby asked, taking another step closer to Aaron. Gage noticed she purposefully stayed to the side, as if ready to jump into the path of a bullet should he begin to shoot.

From the corner of his eye, Gage thought he saw movement behind a couple of the parked cars. Cops?

Please, Lord, help us!

"Mommy!" Leo's abrupt cry startled Aaron.

Gage instantly hit the horn. "Get down!"

Darby dropped to the ground as several cops rushed

forward with their guns raised. "Put the gun down!" a cop shouted at Aaron.

Aaron's weapon turned toward Darby.

"No!" Edith screamed and jumped forward as Aaron pulled the trigger. The cop fired at Aaron, hitting him in the abdomen.

Aaron screamed as he stumbled backward beneath the impact of the bullet. Darby crawled to Edith as the cops surrounded Aaron.

Gage quickly joined Darby and Edith, raking his gaze over them, searching for blood. "Are you hurt?"

"H-he missed," Edith wheezed. She put a hand to her chest. "I-I don't know how, but he missed."

"God was watching over us," Darby whispered. She looked up at him. "Right?"

"Right." He wanted to gather Darby into his arms, but Leo's crying tore at him. He spun toward the car and reached inside for his son.

Gage carried Leo over to Darby and Edith. As they held each other, Gage closed his eyes and thanked God for watching over them.

This time, their nightmare was really over.

CHAPTER SIXTEEN

Darby clutched Gage, Leo, and Edith, willing her heart rate to return to normal. She'd felt the bullet whizz past her face and knew if Aaron had aimed just a quarter of an inch toward her, she'd be dead.

Dead.

Aaron's attempt to kill her had been far closer than what she'd experienced with Reyes. In fact, she honestly had no idea how the bullet had missed her. She'd prepared herself for the pain, but it never came.

It was as if God had intervened in the nick of time.

"Are you sure you're okay?" Gage's voice rumbled near her ear.

"Yes." She turned to watch as two cops handcuffed Aaron while offering first aid to his abdominal wound. "How did the police know we were here?"

"I called Pride without Aaron knowing," Gage admitted. "It worked with Reyes, so I gave it another try. I felt certain he was still close by."

"You thought right." Detective Pride strode toward them. "Is this the guy who stole the black Ford?"

"Yes," Darby answered. "Looking back, I should have recognized him. That's Aaron Dukes, an old boyfriend." One she'd barely given a second thought other than to be thankful she'd gotten rid of him.

Too bad Aaron hadn't done the same.

"Great." Pride sighed. "Two crime scenes in one day."

"Thanks for coming so quickly," Gage spoke up.

Pride gave a curt nod. "I was outside getting ready to leave when your call came through. When I realized you were being held at gunpoint, I saw the parking structure across the street. One of the cops mentioned seeing the four of you heading in that direction." His gaze fell on the whining, bleeding Aaron. "I have to admit, I didn't suspect he'd be here, waiting for you."

"Me either." Darby blew out a breath. Should she have anticipated this? She hadn't even recognized Aaron as the driver of the stolen truck.

So much for her keen observation skills.

"He mentioned having friends in high places," Gage said. "Like maybe a cop."

Pride flushed. "I'll check into it."

"Please do." Darby was shaken by the second near miss in mere hours. "It's the only explanation as to how we've constantly been found."

"We need to know who tampered with the zip line cable," Gage added. "Dukes or Reyes. Hopefully, you can play one off the other to get the information."

"Yeah, but I'm not sure which one of these guys is the worst offender."

Darby shook her head. "I hate to say this, but they're both equally bad. Aaron's grudge against me was far more personal because we were once together." It pained her to admit her youthful foolishness. "But Reyes had the eyes of a killer."

"This will likely be a case of whoever talks first gets the deal." The detective turned toward Aaron. "You hear that? Whoever talks first gets the better deal."

"I've been shot," Aaron whined.

"You almost shot me," Darby snapped back. "So quit complaining. You brought this on yourself, Aaron. We told you to get away before the cops arrived."

"Easy." Gage put a hand on her arm. "He's not worth your anger."

"Reyes loosened the zip line cable," Aaron abruptly confessed. "He wanted Darby and Gage to suffer for turning him in to the cops."

Darby couldn't believe Aaron had given Reyes up so easily. Well, actually she could. After all, Pride was right in that the first person to talk got the better deal.

Wasn't that why she'd turned Gage in to the authorities?

"How do you know Officer Crow?" Gage asked.

"He was my . . ." Aaron abruptly stopped. "I want my lawyer."

Pride's expression turned even more grim. He turned away and spoke into his phone, hopefully putting the rest of the Knoxville police officers on alert about Crow's connection to Aaron Dukes. Darby was glad to know Gage's instincts were right about the guy.

And she wished desperately that Pride had listened to them from the beginning.

All because she'd betrayed Gage all those years ago.

Gage must have been able to read her thoughts. "Don't worry about what happened in the past. I told you, going to jail was the best thing that happened to me."

"That sounds just as insane as the first time you told me that," she admitted. Leo had stopped crying, but he clung to Gage as if he might never let go.

Darby couldn't blame the little boy. She wanted to do the same thing.

But of course they both had jobs to get back to. She was scheduled to work the weekend, and she knew Gage had to be back to work on Monday. Now that Reyes and Aaron had been arrested, and Pride believed them about Officer Crow, they could head home.

Their time together was over. At least for now.

However, she and Gage still needed to discuss custody arrangements. With the danger now over, they'd settle back into their normal routines. Well, a new normal routine, one that included allowing Gage to spend time with Leo. It would probably be a good idea for Gage to spend the weekend with Leo. After all, she'd be at work.

But she'd already spent so much time away from her son, she hated the idea of leaving him again so soon. Yet she also needed to pay for a replacement vehicle, so taking additional time off work wasn't a viable option.

All because these men had wanted revenge.

"Tell me what happened." Pride didn't bother to interview them separately. Darby explained first, and Gage filled in some additional details. Edith didn't have much to add. Once Pride had what he needed, he allowed them to leave.

Soon they were on the road heading back to East Knoxville. Gage was driving, Edith and Leo were tucked into the back seat. Gage had insisted they return to the townhouse. Darby didn't put up any resistance to that plan.

She stared out the window, trying to get a grip on her emotions. After being on edge for days, it felt strange to be sitting calmly and doing nothing.

"Are you okay?" Gage asked in a low voice. "You still look upset.

"Yeah." She glanced at him. "Wouldn't you be upset? I had no idea Aaron was harboring that much resentment toward me and toward you. If I had known, we could have added him as a suspect sooner." She thought again of how much Hailey had hated Aaron and knew that her foster sister had been right about him all along.

"Let's focus on moving forward," Gage suggested.

She drew in a deep breath. "Okay. I, uh, was thinking you could stay at the townhouse with us for a few days."

"Really?" He looked surprised by the offer.

"I'll sleep on the sofa," she added quickly, lest he get the wrong idea. "And I have to work this weekend, which makes it a perfect time for you to hang out with Leo."

"You should take the weekend off," Gage said. "After everything you've been through, a few days of relaxing wouldn't hurt."

"I have to replace my car." She glanced over her shoulder at Edith, who was resting her head against the window with her eyes closed. Guilt hit at how she'd exposed the woman she loved like a mother to danger. Not once, but twice in one day. "I can borrow this one for a while, but not forever."

"I can drive you to and from work this weekend, but I'll have to head back on Sunday afternoon." Gage glanced at her. "We have a lot to talk about."

"We do." She offered a wan smile. "But we'll figure it out."

Gage fell silent as Edith's Lumina ate up the miles from Asbury to East Knoxville. By the time they reached the townhouse, it was nearly dinnertime. Gage offered to grab takeout, but Darby threw a couple of frozen pizzas into the oven.

Leo chattered throughout dinner, seemingly better now that they were home. Darby prayed he wouldn't have nightmares from what he'd experienced today.

"Actually, why don't you sleep in Leo's room?" Darby glanced at Gage as they cleaned up after dinner. "Leo might be better off staying with me tonight."

"That's fine." Gage glanced over to where Leo was playing. Edith had excused herself after dinner to go to bed early. "Anything to help out."

"I'll need to know your schedule so we can discuss which times will be best for you to visit Leo." She turned toward him. "And I know it won't be convenient, driving back and forth from your place to here. I can offer to meet you halfway on my days off."

"No."

She gaped. "What do you mean, no?"

Gage slowly shook his head. "I don't want to just see Leo once a week. I want to be a part of his life."

The blood drained from her face. Had she misjudged Gage? Was he going to fight her for joint custody of their son? She took a step back, and another.

"I think it's time for you to leave." She tried to sound firm, but she wanted to burst into tears.

This wasn't what she'd envisioned. And now she knew the main reason Gage had been so nice to her.

It was all an act to get to Leo.

GAGE FROWNED, trying to understand what was going through Darby's mind. "Leave? I thought you wanted me to stay the weekend?"

"Not anymore." Darby took another step away from him. "If you think I'm giving you joint custody of Leo, you're sadly mistaken."

Joint custody? He mentally smacked himself upside the head. "No, of course not. That's not what I'm asking for."

She narrowed her gaze. "Sure sounded like it."

He'd handled this badly. "Darby, I love you."

"Ha. Yeah, sure. Now you're saying what you think I want to hear in order to get more time with Leo."

He'd really, really handled this badly. He took a step toward her. "Of course I want to spend time with my son. But I would never lie to you about my feelings. Despite the danger, seeing you again has been wonderful. I've never forgotten you, Darby. I stayed away since getting out of jail because I was an ex-con who didn't have anything to offer you." He hesitated, then added truthfully, "And I wasn't sure you were still clean either. The conditions of my parole require me to stay away from drugs and violence, anything that resembles my former life."

Her gaze narrowed. "I'm supposed to believe you would have sought me out sooner?"

"Yes." He held her gaze. "I've always cared about you, but these past few days have made me realize how much I love you. How much I want to be a part of your life, as well as Leo's." He held out his hand. "Won't you please at least give us a try?"

She looked uncertain. "These past few days weren't exactly real life, Gage. I mean, the danger was real, but our being thrown together, working together, wasn't under normal circumstances. How do you know we're compatible?"

"Our kisses are proof we're more than compatible," he replied with a smile. "But I can tell you're not ready, and that's okay. I guess I shouldn't have rushed you." He did his best not to look hurt. He'd thought they were on the same page, especially those moments he'd held her in his arms, but clearly that was not the case.

"I suppose you think God brought us together."

He nodded. "Yes, I do. I think God brought us together seven years ago too. I think God knew we had to work through our past issues before we could move on. Prison helped me to do that. I believe your stay in rehab did the same for you."

"Maybe," she agreed. "Although it seems odd that God would bring two criminals together."

"We're all sinners, Darby. And God knows us better than we know ourselves." He took another step closer. "Please give me a chance. I can't even imagine what my life would be like without you."

"You mean without Leo," she corrected.

"Without you and Leo, yes." He didn't appreciate her thinking the worst of him. "If you aren't interested in having a relationship with me, then I'll agree to seeing Leo once a week. Maybe on Sundays since that's my only day off. I tend to work half days on Saturdays, but I can probably give up those hours if needed."

Her brow furrowed. "You're saying you'd give up time with Leo for me?"

"I'd give my life for you, Darby. The same way you placed yourself in danger for Leo." He held her gaze. "Because you love him."

Her mouth dropped open. "I—see."

"Do you?" He reached out to grasp her hand. "I love you, Darby Walsh. I want to share my life with you."

"Me?" She tightened her grip on his hand. "You're not just saying that?"

"I promise I won't lie to you. Not now, not ever."

She rested her free hand on his chest. "I won't lie to you either. And you don't have to wait that long because I care about you too."

A flicker of hope burned in his chest. "Yeah?"

Her lips curved into a smile. "Yeah."

He drew her toward him. She didn't resist, coming into his embrace and lifting herself up on her tiptoes to kiss him.

As before, their kiss was explosive. More intense than what he'd remembered in the past. Darby felt so right in his arms, as if this was exactly where they were supposed to be.

Together. As a family.

Gage didn't want to let her go. He kissed her until they couldn't breathe, then buried his face in her hair.

"Are you kissing Mommy?" Leo asked.

Their son's innocent question made him grin. Truthfully, he'd almost forgotten Leo was still awake. "Yes, I am. Because I love your mommy very much."

The little boy's gaze shifted between the two of them. "Does Mommy love you too?"

"Uh, well . . ." He tried to think of a way to explain the complexity of their situation.

"Yes," Darby said. "I love your daddy very much."

"What about me?" Leo asked.

Gage laughed and loosened his grip on Darby just enough to reach out to the boy. He lifted the child until he was part of their three-way embrace. "We both love you, too, Leo."

"Yes," Darby whispered. "Mommy and Daddy love you very much."

Leo rested his head on Gage's shoulder. Gage felt his heart swell as he met Darby's soft gaze. "Are you sure? I don't want to rush you into something you're not ready for."

"I'm sure." She kissed Leo's cheek, then his. "I'm sorry I misunderstood your intent, Gage. It just seems like you could do so much better than a former drug addict."

"Hey, I'm an ex-con," he reminded her. "But we are also God's children. And with His love and guidance, we fit perfectly together."

"You're right," Darby admitted softly. "We're better together. I know God must have been watching over us today. I really thought I was going to die."

He tightened his grip around her waist. "Me too. And God answered our prayers, bringing us safely out of danger to this moment right now."

"Yes, I believe He did," Darby whispered. "I guess I'm glad to know the Preacher was wrong all those years ago. That there is a loving and caring God watching over us."

"Ah, Darby." He wanted to kiss her again. "You have no idea how happy I am to hear you say that."

She stroked a hand down Leo's back. "I want Leo to grow up believing in God too. Can you help us with that?"

"I would love to," he assured her.

"Your friend James is the assistant pastor at your church, right?" Darby asked.

"Yes."

She drew in a deep breath. "I haven't been in a church in a long time."

He frowned. "If you're talking about the years since you've escaped the Preacher, please know that wasn't really church. Not God's church."

"I'll try to keep that in mind. But you need to know it may take me a while to be comfortable in a church setting." Darby's blue eyes begged for understanding. "I have tried to move beyond the memories, but it's not easy. Sometimes they return without warning."

He realized she was talking about flashbacks. "Darby, you don't have to go into church until you're ready. In fact, they often have outdoor services when the weather is nice. Maybe not now, in the heat of summer, but come fall, I think they'll start back up again."

"Outdoor services?" A wistful expression crossed her features. "That sounds nice."

"I love you," he repeated.

"And I love you too," Darby assured him.

Gage continued to hold Leo and Darby close as he silently thanked God for bringing them together. For knowing they were better together.

His true family. Now and forever.

EPILOGUE

Two weeks later . . .

Darby walked into the townhouse, surprised to see Gage had already arrived. On these rare nights they were together, Darby encouraged Edith to take some time for herself. Tonight, Edith and a friend of hers had decided to go see a movie. "Hi, you're early. I'll be ready for dinner soon."

"I have news." Gage set Leo on his feet and crossed over to meet her. "I found Hailey Donovan."

She instinctively took a step back. "You did? How? When?"

Now Gage looked uncertain. "I thought you'd be happy. You mentioned wanting to see your foster siblings, so I set out to find Hailey. She lives in Gatlinburg."

"I am happy." She swallowed hard. "And nervous. I don't know what Hailey will think of me." She glanced at their son. "Or Leo."

"I don't think she's going to be upset to learn she's an aunt," Gage said.

"Gatlinburg." Darby realized that neither one of them

had ended up staying in Pigeon Forge. The place was a terribly gaudy tourist attraction these days, worse now than it had been ten years ago.

"I have her phone number," Gage continued. He held out his cell phone. "Call her."

She looked at the phone as if it were a poisonous spider. "How on earth did you get her number?"

"Well, if you must know, she actually found you. Found us. Apparently, our names hit the newspapers, and she had Sawyer help track us down," Gage explained. "She called Detective Pride, who gave her number to me."

Darby took the phone and glanced down at the number Gage had on the screen. She drew in a deep breath and pushed the button.

"Hello?" Hailey's familiar voice caused a visceral reaction. Darby's knees went weak, and she sank onto the sofa.

"Hailey?" Darby's voice was thick with emotion. "Is that you?"

"Yes, is this Darby?"

"Yeah." She gripped the phone so tight she feared she'd crack the casing.

"Is it really you?" Hailey's voice sounded hopeful. "Tell me something only the two of us know."

"We sneaked into motels to eat continental breakfasts." Darby caught Gage's gaze and smiled. "I can't believe we're talking after all this time."

"Oh, Darby, I've thought of you so often." Hailey sighed. "I'm so sorry we argued. I tried to find you after I got out . . ."

"But I'd taken off with Aaron, which turned out to be a big mistake."

"No, it's my fault, I shouldn't have pushed," Hailey

insisted. There was a pause before Hailey asked, "How are you doing?"

"I'm really good. I, uh, got rid of Aaron and, well, made a bunch of other mistakes, but I'm six years sober and doing very well."

"I'm so happy for you."

"I, uh, also have a five-year-old son, Leo. He's a great kid, and I've recently reconnected with his father."

"Darby, listen, you don't have to depend on Leo's father for support. You can relocate here to Gatlinburg, and I'll be happy to help out."

"You're still trying to fix me, huh?" Darby swiped at her tears. "There's no need to worry, Gage Killion is a wonderful guy and believes God brought us together."

"Really? He said that?" Hailey asked.

"Yes." Darby wished she could see the expression on her sister's face. "I love him, Hailey. And he loves me. We're currently in Knoxville. You should know that relocating to Gatlinburg isn't an option."

"I'm really happy you found love, Darby. And, uh, I did too."

It was Darby's turn to be taken by surprise. "Really?"

"I'm engaged to a wonderful man named Rock Wilson, he's a park ranger. And we're hoping to get married very soon."

"That sounds wonderful, Hailey." Darby smiled at Gage. "I hope I get to meet him sometime."

"Oh, you will. I recently returned from Chattanooga, where Sawyer lives. Can you believe he's engaged to be married too? It's kinda crazy when you think about it. So far the three of us have found each other and love."

"Sawyer?" Darby's heart quickened. "Have you found the other fosters too? Cooper, Trent, Jayme, and Caitlyn?"

"Not yet, but we will." Darby could hear Hailey say something in the background. "Listen, Darby, I want to see you. Rock says he'd love to take a weekend trip to Knoxville."

"I'd love to see you too." Darby could hardly believe she was having this conversation. "I've missed you so much, Hailey."

"I've missed you too." Hailey's voice was thick. "You don't know how much I've thought about you over the years."

"Back at you," Darby assured her. "We'll talk soon, okay? You have Gage's number but take mine too." She rattled off the information. "It's wonderful to hear you're happy."

"And I'm glad to hear you're happy too." Hailey sniffed. "I also can't wait to meet my nephew."

Darby laughed. "Soon," she promised. "We'll meet up very soon."

"Love you."

"Love you too." Darby blinked away fresh tears as she handed Gage his phone back. "That was the nicest gift anyone has ever given me."

"Well, I hope I can change your mind about that." Gage gestured for Leo to come over. The little boy stood next to his father, and the likeness between them made her heart melt. "We bought you something, didn't we, Leo?"

The boy nodded and held out a small box. "Daddy and I wanted to buy you something pretty."

"Something pretty?" She took the box, searching Gage's expression. When she opened the box, she saw a modest engagement ring.

"Darby, Leo gave me permission to ask you to marry

me." Gage looked serious. "We can have a long engagement, if that's what you want."

"No, Gage, I don't want a long engagement." She handed him the box. "Put the ring on for me."

He did as she asked, and she nodded. "I love you, Gage, and I'd be honored to be your wife."

"I'm glad to hear that," Gage said. "See, Leo? It worked. Your mommy has agreed to marry me."

"Does that mean we'll live together?" Leo asked.

"Yes, it does," Darby assured him. She hugged and kissed Leo, then threw herself into Gage's arms.

She couldn't remember ever being this happy. Hearing from Hailey and her fiancé, Rock, learning about Sawyer's engagement, followed by Gage's proposal.

Life couldn't possibly get any better than this.

THANKS FOR READING *Darby's Decision*! I hope you're enjoying all the stories related to the foster siblings. Are you ready to meet Cooper and Mia? Read *Cooper's Choice* by clicking here!

DEAR READER

I hope you enjoyed *Darby's Decision,* the third book in my Smoky Mountain Secrets series. I really wanted to write a series featuring characters that have every reason not to believe in God, yet who each find their faith and love.

I'm working hard on *Cooper's Choice,* which will be followed by *Trent's Trust* and *Jayme's Journey.* All six of these books will be published this year. You won't want to miss a single one.

If you enjoyed this book, please consider leaving a review. Reviews are critical to authors, and I would appreciate you taking the time to help me out. Also, I adore hearing from readers. I can be found on Facebook at https://www.facebook.com/LauraScottBooks, via Twitter at https://twitter.com/laurascottbooks, and through my website https://www.laurascottbooks.com. You may want to sign up for my monthly newsletter where I announce new releases along with bargain books from some of my friends. I also offer a free novella that is not for sale on any platform.

If you're interested in Cooper's story, I've attached the first chapter here for your reading pleasure.

Take care and stay safe!
Until next time,
Laura Scott

COOPER'S CHOICE

Cooper Orchard caught a glimpse of the pretty dark-haired woman walking swiftly toward the church for the second day in a row. He'd noticed her for several reasons—her beauty, her single-minded determination, and the air of fragile innocence that surrounded her. His artistic eye had especially longed to capture the intense expression on her heart-shaped face framed by her dark wavy hair.

Turning over the page of his sketchbook, he continued drawing her likeness from what he'd started yesterday, working swiftly as he suspected she wouldn't be there long. At least, she hadn't been yesterday. As her image bloomed on the page, he found himself wondering why she kept going into the church. Two days in a row seemed like a lot.

After suffering physical and psychological abuse during the five long years he'd been stuck living with the Preacher, Cooper had absolutely no desire to get anywhere near the so-called house of God. He refused to have anything to do with religion. The Preacher's screaming about sin and God's wrath had only reinforced the hell he and his foster siblings had lived in. They'd only managed to escape the seemingly endless abuse because of the fire that had broken out late one night.

The Preacher and his wife, Ruth, had died in the blaze. Personally, Cooper had always thought they'd gotten exactly what they'd deserved. Karma, considering how much the Preacher had screamed at them, hitting them with switches as he ranted about the fires of hell.

Well, the fires of hell had certainly taken the Preacher.

He was so intent on his sketch he didn't notice the woman who approached from his left. "Oh, you do such amazing work," she gushed.

Normally, Coop would have turned on the charm. After all, he earned a living by sketching tourists, and August in Gatlinburg was a peak time for business. Women like this lady standing next to him tended to flirt with him, wanting to see their likeness recreated, especially when he made sure their image was more flattering than reality. No wrinkles, no lines, more definition to the cheekbones and jaw. And he always played up their eyes.

Only, today he found himself irritated by the distraction. He forced a smile. "Happy to sketch you after I finish this one."

"And how long will that be?" She sounded a bit put off. As if he should drop everything to cater to her wishes. Again, something he'd normally do.

"An hour, maybe less." He told himself he was crazy to put off a paying customer, but he suspected his mystery girl would be coming out of the church again soon. And he wanted to get another look at her so he could finish his drawing.

"I'll see if I can make it back here." The woman who looked old enough to be his mother turned away.

He let her go and continued drawing, one eye glued to

the church entrance. When the beautiful woman came out of the church, his heart kicked up a notch. There was something about her that called to him. Some quality he couldn't quite define.

Who was she? Why did she go inside the church these past two days? It wasn't even Sunday, although he knew some people didn't limit their worship to one day a week. The Preacher who'd tormented him and his foster siblings had done so nearly every day, rain or shine.

A movement behind his mystery girl made him frown. A man wearing black jeans, a black T-shirt, and a black baseball cap pulled low over his eyes stepped out from behind a tree, falling into step just a few yards behind her. A warning tingle shot down the back of Cooper's neck, every instinct going on high alert. He tossed his charcoal stick down and left his easel, stool, and sketchbook to follow.

At some level, Cooper knew he was taking a risk leaving the tools of his trade behind. After all, drawing was his livelihood. He couldn't afford to replace whatever someone decided to steal. But the man dressed in black appeared to be keeping a keen eye on the pretty woman, and Cooper didn't like it.

He'd lived on the streets long enough to recognize someone with less than honorable intentions when he saw one. When he noticed the pretty woman glancing furtively over her shoulder, he quickened his pace.

The guy in black moved faster too. Cooper instinctively knew the guy intended to grab her. He broke into a run and forcefully rammed into the guy, knocking him off his feet.

"Run," he shouted to the pretty girl as the guy in black scrambled up to take a swing at him.

Cooper ducked and lashed out with his foot, kicking the guy below the belt. Street fighting at its best. The guy in black moaned and doubled over in pain. It was the break Cooper needed.

He rushed forward, irritated to note the pretty girl was standing there, gaping at him in surprise. He scowled. "I told you to run."

"I—you . . ." She looked badly shaken. She belatedly turned and ran.

Cooper kept pace, covering her back. He could practically taste the girl's fear as she sent furtive glances at him over her shoulder.

"Get away from me," she shouted.

She wanted him to get away from her? What about the guy dressed in black? Cooper was no threat. Not like that guy.

Suddenly another man appeared, stepping out from between two buildings. He was dressed exactly like the other guy, all in black including the same plain black baseball cap. The pretty girl gasped and tried to dart around him, but the stranger reached out to snag her arm. She screamed, and Cooper sprinted forward.

"Let her go!" He punched the guy in the face, causing pain to shoot through his hand and up his arm. Not the smartest move as his hands were his bread and butter. The stranger reared back and must have loosened his hold on the pretty girl's arm enough that she was able to yank free.

Cooper followed up with a kick to his groin, before spinning away and once more following the pretty girl. This time, she seemed relieved to see him.

"This way." Cooper grabbed her hand, tugging her around the corner. He knew this area of Gatlinburg better than most from living off the streets and working the tourist crowd. He captured the girl's hand, tugging her to a narrow alley between two buildings.

She went along with him, her dark eyes wide with fear. Cooper took every shortcut he could think of to put more distance between them and the two men dressed in black.

He finally led her into a coffee shop located two blocks from his low-budget apartment. He figured the coffee shop would put her at ease more so than taking her to his private digs.

"W-who are you?" she managed when they snagged an empty table near the window.

"Cooper Orchard. Who are you?"

"Mia . . ." She stopped, bit her lip, and glanced away. "Thanks for your help. I should go."

"Wait a minute." He held up his hand. "Shouldn't you call the police? Those guys were about to grab you."

"I-I will." She glanced around nervously. "But you need to stay far away from me."

He stared at her. Mia was a pretty name, but he had a feeling it wasn't her real one. Not that he was one to talk. His last name was fake too. As was his ID, driver's license, and social security number. "I think it's a little late for that. I just assaulted two men."

"I'm sorry." Her expression crumpled. "Truly, I feel terrible you had to do that. But this isn't your problem. Thanks for your help, but you should go back to your sketching."

He lifted a brow. "You noticed me sketching?"

She blushed, then frowned. "Go away, Cooper. Leave me alone."

He didn't understand what was going on with her, but no way could he simply walk away. He raked his gaze over her arms, relieved there were no needle tracks marring her skin. Prostitution? Sex trafficking? Maybe.

"Let's head over to the closest police station. They'll

help you get away from those guys, find you a safe place to stay."

"I can't." Her voice was a mere whisper.

He swallowed a wave of frustration. "The cops aren't going to arrest you." At least, he didn't think so. Then again, he wasn't sure what she was running from. Had she committed some terrible crime? Armed robbery? Manslaughter?

Murder?

It seemed unlikely, especially since her fear was too real to be faked. She must be a victim. So why not go to the cops?

"You don't understand." She slid off the stool. "Really, Cooper, I appreciate your help. But you're better off staying far away from me."

The smart move would be to let her go. To return to his sketching, hoping no one had stolen his stuff. He had rent to pay. Sitting here with Mia wasn't going to bring in the cash he needed to live.

But he couldn't walk away. Not from a woman in distress. "Okay, look. I'll take you to my apartment. You can stay there while I go back for my things. We'll figure out where to go from there, okay?"

Mia shook her head. "You don't know what you're getting into."

No, he didn't. Although it was obvious Mia was running from a couple of bad dudes. Two men he'd assaulted, not that he believed either one of them would report the incidents to the police.

Mia was in danger, and he couldn't stand the idea of something bad happening to her. It was oddly reassuring that she kept trying to protect him. "I live nearby." He met her gaze. "Don't you think the best move right now is to hide out for a while? Disappear long enough to shake those guys loose?"

She hesitated, clearly torn between wanting to do just that and staying on the move. He could relate as he'd spent several months avoiding the police while struggling to survive. He and Trent had spent several years on the streets, before Cooper began using his sketching to make money legitimately from tourists rather than stealing from them.

Sketching didn't pay as well, but he preferred working than running. Trent had gotten involved with a band, and for a while they'd continued to live together. Until the band had moved on to Nashville.

It had hurt Cooper to lose the company of his foster brother, but he'd made the best choice for his own well-being. Trent had done the same. He couldn't blame Trent for taking a different path, for wanting something more. Even if that meant leaving Cooper behind.

He shook off the depressing thoughts. "Mia? My place?" It struck him she might be thinking the worst. "I'll sleep on the couch. I promise I won't take advantage of the situation."

"And I should believe you, why?"

He liked the fighting spirit in her dark eyes. "Good point, we really don't know each other. To be honest, there is something I'd like from you."

Her entire body went tense. "No."

He shook his head. "You didn't let me finish. I'd like to sketch you."

She frowned. "Why on earth do you want to do that?"

"I'm an artist, and you're beautiful," he answered honestly. "Just a sketch, nothing more, in exchange for you being able to hide out from those bad guys who tried to abduct you."

She was silent for several long moments. Finally, she nodded. "Okay. A sketch."

"Great." Relief intermingled with anticipation washed over him. Mia had agreed to stay, at least for the night.

Technically, he'd lied about what he'd wanted from her. He wanted to understand what was going on, who she was running from, and why. He also wanted to protect her, which was a bit unusual, especially for someone who'd spent years looking after himself.

But for now, he'd settle for the sketch.

WHAT IN THE world was she doing with Cooper Orchard?

Mia Royce knew she should find a way to ditch him. She was safer on her own. Well, maybe not, but Cooper was definitely much safer without her.

She was the one in danger. She had no right to drag an innocent guy into her problems. Into the mess that was her life.

Yet the chance of having a safe place to stay for a few hours had been too good to pass up. She'd called her US Marshal contact, Sean McCarthy, yesterday as scheduled, but she hadn't heard back.

Which was strange as usually Sean responded very quickly to her calls for help.

Witness protection, better known as WITSEC, wasn't all it was cracked up to be. How had Frank Germaine's men found her so quickly?

The church.

She inwardly winced at the thought. There was more than one church in Gatlinburg, but apparently

Germaine's men had watched each of them in an effort to find her.

A tactic that had obviously worked.

Sean had counseled her not to go back to her old habits. That doing such a thing would make it easier for them to find her. And he'd been right.

Yet she needed God's strength and support. Her faith was all she had left. Everyone else was gone. Dead or gone in a way she'd never see them again.

Lord, I need You. Please keep me safe.

"Mia?" Cooper's voice interrupted her thoughts.

"What?"

"Are you sure about this? I don't want you to be afraid."

It was far too late for that. Germaine's men scared her more than anything on the planet. The irony was that Cooper didn't scare her at all. He was a stranger, yet she still wasn't frightened of him. Maybe because she'd seen him sketching on the sidewalk across from the church over the past two days. She glanced through the window. "You think it's safe to head outside?"

"We'll go out the back, I know one of the kitchen workers." Cooper stood and held out his hand. He was incredibly handsome, wearing his blond hair longer than most men she'd known, his overall appearance being that of a magazine model rather than an artist. His topaz gaze was mesmerizing, she'd felt its impact even from a distance.

She took his hand, doing her best to ignore the zing of attraction. This was hardly the time or the place for such foolishness. Her plan was to stay with Cooper for one night. She'd sleep on his sofa and hopefully hear back from Sean McCarthy. The US Marshals would show up and escort her to yet another city, providing her yet another name.

The idea filled her with despair, but there wasn't

another option. She'd testified against Frank Germaine. Now his son, Frankie Junior, was determined to make her pay.

With her life.

Cooper guided her through the kitchen to the rear door of the shop. She was mildly surprised no one stopped them or asked what they were doing. Cooper must do this sort of thing on a regular basis.

Or maybe he came back here to see his *friend* on a regular basis. There had been two younger women working back there, both very pretty. Cooper looked like the type of guy who could have his pick of women.

He may have called her beautiful, but she knew that was likely a line. Something to convince her to let him sketch her. Maybe he needed practice or something.

The apartment building was small and could have used a bit of maintenance. Not that she was living in the lap of luxury these days.

Once, she'd gone to private schools and lived in the largest house in the neighborhood. Before she'd discovered her father was doing business with Frank Germaine. Illegal business.

Criminal activity that had ultimately gotten her father and stepmother murdered. Leaving her as the only witness to the crime.

"It's nothing fancy." Cooper had mistaken her silence for disapproval.

"It's perfect." She smiled. "Thanks for doing this. I really appreciate having a place to hang out for a while."

His gaze bored into hers. "For a while? Will you still be here when I return with my things?"

She hesitated, then nodded. "Yes. I won't lie to you. My being here puts you in danger. But I promise I won't leave without telling you." Being honest was the least she could do.

"Okay. Thanks." Cooper waved a hand to the miniscule kitchen. "Help yourself. I should be back within the hour."

"I will." She watched him go, then pulled out her disposable phone. The one Marshal Sean McCarthy had given her. When her second call went unanswered, her stomach twisted painfully, and she sank down onto the sofa.

Something was wrong. Terribly wrong. Germaine's men shouldn't have found her here in Gatlinburg, and Marshal Sean should be answering his phone and making plans to come whisk her to safety.

The US Marshals had assured her she'd be safe with them. Explaining how they'd never lost a witness who followed their rules. The most important being not to contact anyone in her former life.

Not a single person, a friend, old college roommate, old boyfriend. No one.

And she had followed their rules. She'd cut off all ties to everyone she'd known back in Chicago. The only rule she'd broken was going to church. It was the one former habit she hadn't been able to stop.

Logically, she hadn't viewed going to church services to be a big problem since her location and identity here in Gatlinburg was supposed to be a secret.

A decision that had backfired in a big way. Her secret location was anything but. Germaine's men had found her. How? She had no clue.

What if something had happened to Sean? The marshal wasn't that old, maybe ten years her senior, but maybe he had an aneurysm. Or an aggressive form of cancer. A sudden heart attack.

She stood and paced the small length of the room.

Every possibility that flashed through her mind was worse than the previous one.

Maybe Frankie Junior had found Sean and killed him to get the marshal out of the way. Leaving no one left to protect her. Had they known her contact with the US Marshals had been limited to Sean McCarthy? That in order to be safe no one else within the organization knew where she was? That she didn't have another person to contact?

How long would it take the US Marshals service to realize something happened to Sean? How long before another marshal reached out to her?

Too long, considering Frankie Germaine's men had already found her in Gatlinburg.

Which meant she had little choice but to get out of town, the sooner the better.

Before Germaine's men could find her for a second time and make another attempt to kill her.

Manufactured by Amazon.ca
Acheson, AB